BOURBON BLUES

BIJOU HUNTER

Cover Design
Photographer: NAS CRETIVES
Photo Source: Shutterstock
Cover Copyright © 2016 Bijou Hunter

Dedication
Freckles, Tigger, Pooh, and Roo for shining light in a gloomy world.
My own personal Mustang Sally for shaking sense into me on a regular basis.
Saucy Sarah for being a beta reading babe.
Naughty Nicole for making me smile when I want to sulk.
Jazzy Jaimie for brainstorming with my dysfunctional self.

ONE - CAMDEN

I'm a man unaccustomed to sitting on his ass and preaching patience. Call me spoiled, but I want what I want. I grew up as the son of two powerful families in a small town where everyone respected, adored, or feared me. I never knew hardship, so I never learned patience. Not until Daisy Crest.

Two months ago, the bewitching brunette got herself liquored up something fierce, and her inner wild child broke loose at a party. I happened to be there to enjoy the sight and saw the opportunity to snuggle up with the girl I'd only known from a distance.

Less than thirty minutes after I talked her up, our lips devoured each other in the house's tiny bathroom. Sweaty and giggling, Daisy only wanted me, and I was already addicted to her sweet flavor.

Out of nowhere, she flipped the switch on me and ran away like Cinderella bailing from the ball. I watched her disappear into the night, wondering what I'd done to make her run. The next day, I called her up. One message after another went unanswered until I accepted I'd been dissed by the one chick wearing a smile I needed to see.

A more mature man would've handled the situation better. He likely wouldn't have blurted out the cock tease allegations to everyone he saw for the next few days. Immature or not, I'm a man who gets what he wants, and I really wanted Daisy.

I assumed the only reason she'd turned chilly on me was that my cousin is her sister's baby daddy. Ruby and Bonn went down in flames years ago, and the sisters were still holding a grudge against our family.

My bud Bonn was the one to set me straight about the girl who dug her way into my system from a single hot night in the peak of summer.

1

"She's insecure, dickhead," was his helpful reply. "And likely a virgin, so you banging her in the bathroom might have, oh, I don't know, freaked her the fuck out."

Once Bonn explained about Daisy's shyness, the hunt was on. She hasn't blown me off, and I still had a shot with her.

Winning Daisy's affections ought to be easy enough. I scared off any guy foolish enough to show her interest, which wasn't difficult since her taste in men proved pathetic. First, I drove away the gaming nerd. Then, I frightened the salesman with the hideous comb-over and freaky bright white smile. The instructor from a Nashville community college looked like a step up for her, except he had three divorces in his back pocket and crippling alimony payments. Where was she meeting these fuckers?

Online dating was the answer. Apparently, after this sexy biker spooked her two months earlier, Daisy decided to date any repulsive piece of crap who gave her profile a second glance. None of them were worthy of her, so I ran off each one with whatever rumor or scare tactic I could think of.

Daisy seemed none the wiser, but she also refused to return my calls. Bonn claimed he heard through the grapevine she was pissed that I called her a chubby cock tease. While I hadn't said a damn thing about her weight, the insult was somehow added to my original complaint.

With Daisy pissed, I got stuck on the sidelines while she wasted time with online twerps.

Bored with the patience game, I do what any man like me would do. I sneak into the Lush Gardens Trailer Park and siphon the gas from her rundown car. Now, she'll need to take the bus to work. That's when I can white-knight my way back into her good graces and enjoy her perfect smile again.

Unfortunately, Daisy has her own plans.

TWO - DAISY

I blame my diet for why I oversleep. Salad before bed never fools my stomach, and I woke at three with a growling gut. After indulging in a slice of cheese, I return to bed at four. Waking hours later proves difficult, and I stumble around my two-bedroom trailer, trying to get my crap in order. I'd still be on time for work if my car wasn't out of gas.

The Lush Gardens Trailer Park's manager is my mom's best friend's husband. When my red Chevy Lumina Euro Sedan wouldn't start months ago, Billy magically fixed it. Unfortunately, he's a late sleeper, and I can't wake him up just because someone siphoned the gas from my clunker.

My mother and two sisters live in the park, but they've already left for work. After bidding farewell to my three fur-babies and locking up the trailer, I nearly run the two blocks to where I'll grab the first of three buses to get me to my job at the Suds N' Sun Laundry and Tanning.

Waiting for the bus, I study the two grungy guys sitting on the stop's bench. They hem and haw before offering me their space. When I say, "Thank you, but I'm fine," they look relieved. Chivalry isn't dead, but it's lazier.

Chewing wildly on sugar-free gum, I listen to Tears for Fears on my headphones. I'm wearing my usual Tuesday work clothes. With baggy black shorts over black stockings, I finish off my sloppy chic look with a T-shirt and black boots. Back in junior high, I realized I lacked any fashion sense. My older sister Ruby suggested I go hog-wild with my mismatched style choices and pretend I was quirky. A decade later and I was still dressing like a color-blind fashion reject.

Waiting for the bus under the increasingly warm sun, I daydream about one of two obsessions I nurse these days. The first compulsion revolves around how much I miss eating carbs. The second is the blond warrior now riding past me on his giant black Harley like a modern-day Viking. As

3

much as I long for carbs and Camden Rutgers, I detest them for being so bad for me.

Two months ago, I drank too many screwdrivers at Hannah Tripp's birthday party and ended up climbing the giant local sex symbol. Like whenever I drink, things ended badly, and now I'm saddled with the reputation as a cock tease.

No, scratch that. I'm a chubby cock tease, according to Camden. So now, I'm forced to eat lots of rabbit food in my bid to lose the weight I once preferred attached to my curvy ass.

Camden Rutgers ruined my confident woman persona, and now I'm insecure like every other chick in the world. He's a shithead, and I fucking hate him, but there's no denying he's the definition of smoking hot when his Harley circles before heading straight for the bus stop.

Tapping my foot to Duran Duran singing in my ear, I pretend not to notice him. The grungy guys on the bench enjoy donuts, and my stomach growls with jealousy. With so much temptation around me, I look at my phone and ignore Camden's voice calling my name.

He shuts down the Harley and climbs off. Next to me, the guys shrink at the sight of the approaching Hulk. I don't blame them for wetting their boxers. Camden sports a height over six-four along with the wide, thick shoulders of a man capable of carrying their lifeless bodies to whatever shallow grave he has available.

"Hey, you," he says, tapping my head.

"What?" I ask, fully selling my confusion about who this magnificent creature might be. "Are you Dayton or Camden?"

God blessed the world with two versions of the sex mountain before me. Dayton is considered the less mature of the two. But after Hannah's party, Camden sucks pretty hard, too.

"Camden," he mutters, lifting his sunglasses onto his head and pushing back his thick blond mane.

"Oh, hello."

"What are you doing waiting for a bus?"

"Is that a real question?"

"No, I guess not. Want a ride?"

I ought to receive an Oscar for the level of disinterest I sell with my shrug. "No."

"Come on. I'll get you to work faster than any bus."

"No, I'm good."

"It'll be fun."

"No."

"You know you want to."

Frowning, I mutter stronger, "No."

"Sure, you do."

"No."

Camden gives me a smile, and I feel a hot swirl of longing in my gut. How can I defeat a man capable of breaking down my barriers with a single smile?

"Look, you and I both know you'll say yes eventually. Why waste all this time?"

"No."

"I'm a very good driver."

"No."

"I know how to get to your job."

Crossing my arms, I look past him and down the road. "No."

"The bus will be crowded."

"No."

"What are you chewing on?"

Startled by the question, I shrug. "Gum."

"Can I have some?"

"It's sugar-free."

"Why?"

"Because I didn't want sugar."

"But you want a ride, don't you?"

"No."

"It's hot out here," he says, wiping sweat from his thick, tanned neck.

5

"No."

"No, it's not hot?"

"No."

"I sense you're upset. Wanna talk?"

Pulling out my earbuds, I glance at his Harley. "I'm surprised you'd want my fat ass on your precious bike. Aren't you worried I'll break it?"

"And there it is," he says, tugging at the seam of my burgundy sleeveless shirt with the word "GEEK" printed across the front. "I want it stated for the record that I never said anything about your weight. That was all Brittany Sams. You know she has a bug up her ass about your sister, and I guess she figured starting shit about you was just as good as going after Harmony."

The Brittany Sams thing sounds true. All through high school, the bitch hounded Harmony before turning around and claiming Harmony was stalking her. Okay, so maybe the chubby thing wasn't Camden, but...

"Did you call me a cock tease with a frozen pussy?"

Camden awkwardly shifts his stance. "I only called you a cock tease. The rest of that shit was added by troublemakers."

"Poor you," I mutter, glaring at him behind my sunglasses.

"Let me make it up to you by giving you a ride."

"No."

Camden crosses his strong arms and gives me a death glare. "I won't take no for an answer, Daisy Bourbon Crest. Now you need to get your cute ass on my Harley."

"No," I say before frowning at the snickering grungy guys. I don't know if they're amused by his demands or my name, but I return my gaze back to Camden. "Go away."

"I'll pick you up and carry you to the Harley," he threatens while wearing a smile that betrays his anger.

"I wouldn't do that if I were you."

"Why? And don't say something about your weight because I think you look sexy as hell."

I nearly smile at his compliment. After all, I've suffered greatly by losing twenty pounds these last two months. I'd have lost even more if I didn't repeatedly cheat. I blame my mom and sisters. They consume pizza like it's at the bottom of the food pyramid.

"I have to pee," I say when Camden makes a move for me. "If you jiggle me around, I might lose control of my bodily functions."

"Are you threatening to piss on me?"

"Threatening is such an ugly word."

As Camden studies me, his mahogany-colored eyes reveal several emotions. First, he's irritated. Then, he's amused. Finally, he seems curious.

"I'm calling your bluff," he says, reaching for my waist.

"No, fine, I'll get on myself. Just don't touch me."

A triumphant Camden steps aside. I jam my phone and glasses in my stripped backpack before hurrying to his Harley. The bike is as wide as a horse, and I fell off the only horse I've ever ridden.

Camden settles onto his Harley and holds out a hand for me. Ignoring his attempted helpfulness, I fumble onto the bike. His blue shirt stretches across his back in the sexiest way, but I refuse to touch it.

"Babe," he says, looking over his shoulder at me, "I get you're pissed and all that jazz, but if you don't hold onto me, you'll fly off at the first turn. Chances are your mighty anger won't blunt the fall either."

"Okay, but don't take any touching personally."

"Fuck that. If you so much as breathe on me, I'm assuming you want sex."

After rolling my eyes as he laughs at my few attempts to wrap my arms around him, I finally get comfortable.

"Don't drive too fast."

"Okay," he says, turning on his roaring beast.

I clench his shirt in my hands and bury my face in his muscular back. As much as I want to look cool, I'm scared to

7

fall off the Harley. My tolerance for pain is so slim I cry when I trip over my cats and fall on the carpeted floor.

I can't tell if Camden is driving slow or speeding. Either way, my bladder aches in terror. My eyes remain closed since the world flies by too quickly on the Harley like it never does when I drive my crap car.

Minutes later, we arrive at the Suds N' Sun Laundry and Tanning, and I instantly climb off the Harley. Just as quickly, I lose my balance and tumble on my ass.

"Smooth move, Bourbon Babe."

I ignore his outstretched hand and stand on my own. "Thanks for the ride."

"Want me to pick you up? We can go somewhere and talk."

"No."

"Don't start that again."

"Or what?"

Camden lifts an eyebrow, and I wonder if I've challenged his ego.

"Thanks for the ride," I say again.

"Let me pick you up and take you out."

I build up all of the confidence I've accumulated over my twenty-five years and stare right into his perfect eyes.

"Look here, big guy. We had some fun that night, but all the kissing was because of booze, not genuine interest. Why did you think I didn't call you?"

"Because you're shy and figured you embarrassed yourself by running out of the party."

Rolling my eyes, I hate how he's right. "No, because you and I aren't anything except a drunken mistake. Nothing personal. You're not my type any more than I'm yours."

"Babe, you don't know my type."

"Fine. You're not my type."

"Who is?"

I detect a hint of male possessiveness in his question. Camden Rutgers isn't accustomed to men taking his property.

"Shy, goofy guys with dumb hair and overbites."

"That's a pretty fucking specific description. What's the fucker's name?"

"Gaylon Longdong," I say because my brain shorted out from the earlier lying. Camden laughs while I take a step back, but I only mumble, "Thanks again for the ride."

"You keep saying that."

"It's my attempt to ditch you, Camden."

"I think we should go out after work and talk about how I'm a jackass for calling you a cock tease. And how you want to forgive me since I'm a great kisser."

"That's not a good enough reason to forgive," I say, stepping back as if the laundromat's door will provide me freedom from this awkward moment. "Besides, I already forgave you."

"But you can't go out with me because of Longdong?"

"That sounds right."

"Does he kiss you sweet?" Camden asks in a dark voice, challenging my imaginary guy and me.

"No. He has broccoli breath and a dry mouth, but I still like him."

Camden grins. "You want to tell me yes."

"I'm a girl. We're vaginally programmed to say yes to guys like you. That doesn't mean I have to like it."

"I'll pick you up later."

Shocked by his persistence, I blurt out another lie, "My sister is picking me up."

"Ruby or Harmony?"

"Whichever one will scare you off."

Camden stretches like a bear playing with its terrified prey. I spot his belly button when his shirt rides up. I don't know why that image makes my vagina hum with curiosity, but I force my gaze away.

"Here's a twenty for the gas I took," he says, pressing the bill in my hand. "I'll see you after work."

"I won't be here waiting for you."

9

Camden takes a big step and pins me to the door of the laundromat. He stares intensely into my eyes, making me hold my breath.

"I don't want to siphon your gas every morning until you relent. Just do what I say and save us both the trouble of going through this ruse."

Swallowing hard, I muster up a bit more courage, but I feel it running low. "I'd call you a stalker, but I sense you'd take that as a compliment."

"I get what I want."

"Why do you want me now? It's been two months."

"I tried waiting for you to come back to me, but my patience ran out. I'll see you after work."

His body heat infects me, and I want a shower to wash away the uncomfortable desires racing through my every nerve. Rather than reveal my intense attraction—nay, horniness—I shrug.

"You can do whatever you want, Camden Cheesestick Rutgers, but I promise nothing in return."

"That's not my middle name."

"No, not the one your mom gave you."

Camden leans down to kiss me, but I turn my head, and his luscious lips land on my cheek. Warm, moist, and without a hint of broccoli-scent, the momentary affection awakens a part of me dead since Hannah's party. I allow my gaze to meet his when he steps back.

"Thanks for the ride," I say for the hundredth time. "See you around."

Before Camden can make more promises or aim more kisses, I open the door to the laundromat and hide inside. He doesn't leave immediately. In fact, I shove my salad lunch in the office fridge and return to the front counter before hearing his Harley. As much as I want to watch Camden ride away, I refuse to indulge my obsession with the addictive asshole.

THREE - CAMDEN

Hickory Creek Township is my playground, and I never plan to leave. People recognize me when I ride my red Harley named Shasta down the small Tennessee town's streets. I know most of them, too.

Even if I don't know their names, I have a gist of their stories and whether they're threats, allies, or nobodies. As the son of the Serrated Brotherhood MC's president, Adam "Mojo" Rutgers, my future requires knowing everyone and everything. One day, I'll run Hickory Creek Township. While my twin, Dayton, might help, I can never be sure with how his cock runs roughshod over his brain.

My mother, Clara Hallstead, lives in a massive two-story house on a big green piece of land my father bought her as part of their divorce settlement decades earlier. These days, Mom lives with her new husband, Erik, and my half-brother, Hudson. When I pull up to the house, "Medicine" by Tab Benoit blares full blast from the open windows.

Parking Shasta next to Dayton's unnamed Harley, I walk up the porch and into the house where Yipper awaits. Mom's older Pomeranian barks wildly at me even after I pick him up. The dog loves to fucking bark. I've even seen him do it in his sleep.

"Your father is a son of a bitch," Clara announces as I walk into the two-story family room. "I hid that from you boys when you were kids, but you're old enough to hear it now."

"You've been saying that for a long time."

"Well, you've been old enough for the truth for a long time," she says, giving me a wink.

Mom was quite the sexy biker bitch back in the day. I've seen pictures of her with wild blonde hair, short shorts, and blue shadow matching her eyes. Dad claims she was a virgin slut when they met. Of course, I remind him how I

11

choose to never imagine my mother naked EVER. Mojo always laughs and talks more about her hot curves.

"People fuck, Camden. Don't be a stuck-up bitch about it," Mojo likes to say.

Clara remains a looker. Though she's more Hallstead upstanding than Rutgers wild since leaving my father for behaving as the aforementioned son of a bitch.

"What did he do now?" I ask, letting Yipper go so he can run to where my blond, buzz-cut sporting brother, Hudson, stands on the back porch.

"He wants to buy the De Campo's Pizza Shop."

"So?"

"And turn it into a strip bar."

"So?" Dayton asks from the couch where he rests with an arm over his face.

I glance down at my twin brother and find him nursing a hangover. Taking out my phone, I set a loud alarm to go off next to his face.

"You're a dickhead," he growls.

"Why you so angry, bro?" I ask innocently.

Grinning, Dayton hides behind his arm again. He eventually turns over, so his shoulder-length blond hair covers his face.

"Will you talk to him?" Clara asks, tugging me to the kitchen. "I made you a pie."

"He won't listen to me."

"Bullshit," Clara mutters. "You just want another titty bar around here."

"Never for myself. I'm only looking out for those talentless hot women who need jobs. Don't neglect their plight."

Clara gives me a dark look, but I only smile. Not getting her way, she removes the pie from the kitchen island.

"Don't be that way," I say, glancing at the pie over her shoulder. "Is it apple?"

"No, it's cranberry. Go away."

"Fine," I sigh. "I'll talk to him, but I promise no particular result."

Returning the pie to the island, Mom gives me a winning smile. "That's a good boy."

I take out a plate and cut myself a slice. Mom tops it with so much whipped cream I can barely see the actual pastry. She knows just how I like it.

"Do you remember Daisy Crest?" I ask.

"Her father is the ambulance chaser, right?"

"Yeah."

"Her mom, Mustang Sally, used to run in the same party circles as I did years ago. With the way she drinks like a fish, it's no wonder she loves living at Lush Gardens or named her kids after liquor."

"What do you think of Daisy, though?"

Dayton sits up on the couch before grimacing at the bright sun. "Are you chasing the chubby cock tease again?"

Clara sighs. "You boys are so cruel. I blame your father."

Dayton gives me a smile. "You can't start a rumor about a chick and still think she'll want to bang you."

"I do the banging, idiot, and I only started the cock tease thing."

"She was a little chubby."

"No, she was curvy," I growl, ready to punch his handsome face. "I don't like skinny chicks with all their bones jutting out everywhere."

"I'm a skinny chick," Clara says, hands on her hips.

I stare at my mother for nearly a minute before shrugging. "There is no response I can give that won't make me look like an ass."

"No, probably not, Cam."

Dayton leans back on the couch. "Harmony says Daisy hates you."

"What else does Harmony say?"

"She believes in Bigfoot and the Loch Ness Monster."

"She sounds lovely," Clara announces. "Who is Harmony?"

"Daisy's sister."

"You know," Clara murmurs in a conspiratorial tone, "Sally has no luck with marriage, and none of her girls got married, even the two with kids. They're a fertile stock, though. I wouldn't mind having grandkids before I'm too old to deal with the noise."

"Daisy hates him!" Dayton yells, making sure we don't forget his earlier declaration.

"She's angry, but no way does she hate me. Besides, you chase Harmony around, and she's injured you on several occasions."

"She's feisty," Dayton says and then laughs. "She thinks dinosaurs still roam the earth."

Clara gives me an odd look before going to the fridge to pour a glass of milk to go with my pie.

"Why are you interested in Daisy out of all the girls who don't hate you?" she asks.

"Daisy doesn't hate me."

"Why her, baby?"

"I don't know," I mumble, shrugging. "I saw her around and thought she was hot. When she pulled her cock tease move, I got pissed."

"You handled that great, too, bud!" Dayton yells.

"Shut the fuck up!" I yell back.

"No fighting in the house," Clara announces. "Your brother is doing his schoolwork."

I look at where sixteen-year-old Hudson stares out into the backyard while two Pomeranians sit at his feet.

"He's not doing anything."

"He's contemplating life," Clara says without a hint of humor. "He's becoming one with his surroundings."

Dayton sits up enough to share a look with me over the back of the couch. After a mutual eye roll, my brother hides his face again.

"Does Hudson do actual math or reading?"

14

"Sure, but that was earlier. Now, he's meditating. Later, he'll have gun training with his dad," Clara says, walking to the living room where she curls up in a chair. "Don't be jealous your father wouldn't let me homeschool you two."

"I liked school," Dayton says.

"If homeschooling involves meditation, I'm okay with skipping that," I add.

"Send the Daisy girl flowers," Clara says from the living room. "If she's angry, flowers will soften her up."

Dayton snorts his amusement. "I'll ask Harmony what flowers Daisy likes. Betcha they ain't daisies."

"After you do something sweet for your crush," Clara says, "talk to your father about the pizza shop. Mickey doesn't want to sell, but the Brotherhood is strong-arming him."

Hudson enters the room and looks us over. The kid is getting big, and I wouldn't be surprised if he ends up hitting over six-four.

"Extortion is the legal term for what they do," Hudson says.

"Look at the lawman over here," Dayton mumbles and rolls off the couch. "Mom, I'm crashing in the guest room."

"Rest for a few hours. When you get up, I'll make you a sandwich."

I roll my eyes at a grinning Dayton. He loves our mother's babying. While I like her babying me, too, I'm subtle about it.

Hudson joins me at the kitchen island. "Why did you call the girl you like a cock tease?"

"Because she acted like one."

"Didn't you know she'd be upset if you called her that?" Shrugging at his question, I hate when Hudson turns inquisitor. He studies me, and I know he isn't finished with the questions. "Did you not care if she was upset?"

"I cared, but I was pissed."

"Now, she's pissed."

"Yeah, but she'll get over it like I did."

"How long were you pissed?"

"A few weeks," I say, taking my dish to the sink and washing it.

"Why did it take you so long to stop being pissed?"

"I wasn't pissed all that time."

"So, why do you want to buy her flowers now?"

"I'm done waiting for her to chase me."

"So, she needs to stop being pissed because you're impatient?"

"Are you planning to be a lawyer?" I ask, crossing my arms and frowning down at him.

"No, but I like rules and logic."

"The heart ain't about logic, Hud. My heart got stomped on when she blew me off, and I overreacted. Now, my heart is ready to give shit another try."

"What about her heart?"

I recall how angry Daisy was today and figure she's still sore about my tantrum. She let me kiss her cheek when we arrived at her work, so I decide to take that as a good sign.

"I'll fix things," I finally say.

Hudson watches me with his dark eyes, and I watch him with mine. I don't know how he beats me in this staring contest, but I suspect it's only because he has nowhere to go while I have errands to run. Giving up, I walk past him and into the living room where Clara brushes Pip.

"I'll talk to Mojo," I tell her. "Thanks for the pie."

"Get the girl one of those mixed flower bouquets. Roses are too obvious, and daisies will likely make her mad. The mixed ones show you think outside the box."

"Or my mom does."

Clara Hallstead Rutgers Patrick gives me a big smile. "If you want this girl, you'll get this girl. Just don't give up. I made your father work for it, and that made him a better man. This girl can do the same for you," she says and then adds, "Or at least, you'll have fun during the chase."

Leaving behind my mom and siblings, I return to the roads of Hickory Creek Township. Dad wants me to show up

16

at several sites and look scary. I also need to talk to him about the pizza shop and pick up flowers for Daisy.

First, though, I plan to find out if her dry mouth mystery man is the real deal. If he poses a threat to my second chance with Daisy, I'll need to pick up a shovel and pay the guy a visit.

FOUR - DAISY

An hour passes between when Camden drops me off and my cell ringing. I'm technically supposed to avoid talking on the phone at work, but my manager is too busy on hers to notice. I slip away to the dryers and answer the call from Ruby.

"Why were you riding Camden Rutgers's Harley?" she asks rather than saying hello.

"How did you know it was Camden? Could have been Dayton."

"No, Lydia said she saw you riding Shasta, and everyone knows that's Camden's Harley. So, fess up."

Despite my exasperated sigh, I'm relieved to have someone to talk to about Camden. "He siphoned the gas from my car, and I ended up walking to the bus stop where he showed up and offered me a ride."

"Why would you say yes?"

"I didn't until he threatened to pick me up and force me."

"Did you consider using your pepper spray?" Ruby asks, and I sense she's ready to laugh.

"No. Can you even imagine if I used it on Camden? I wonder if he'd kick my ass or pay someone to do it."

"Probably pay someone. I doubt he hits women."

"True."

"So, you're okay?"

"Yeah, how did you find out from Lydia?"

"When she saw you pass by the liquor store she's working at now, she called Mom, who called Harmony and me to see if we knew what was going on."

"Well, now, you do."

"What's his deal?"

I shrug even though Ruby can't see me. "He wanted to apologize for that night and calling me a cock tease."

"What about calling you chubby?"

"He claims Brittany Sams added that part."

"Seems likely. She hates Harmony for being prettier or smelling better. Something ridiculously childish from high school." Remaining silent, I feel my sister working out the situation. "So, what now?"

"I don't know."

"Camden didn't go through all that trouble just to apologize."

"He wants to pick me up after work and go out to talk."

Ruby snorts and says in her throaty voice, "Yeah, talk."

"I want to ditch him, but he'll just chase me. Maybe it's better if I go out with him and be a super dull dorky loser, so he'll ditch me."

"That has the makings of a solid plan, but I worry."

"About what?"

"He's a handsome guy, and he clearly has powers over your common sense."

"I only made out with him at Hannah's party because I was drunk."

"Sure, sure, kitten."

Rolling my eyes at her condescending tone, I ask, "Do you want to come on the date and babysit me, big sis?"

"That's not a bad idea. Harmony and I could bring the kids and sit nearby to provide you with an exit strategy."

"What if he wants to go somewhere that isn't family-friendly?"

"We'll leave the kids with Mom."

"I don't know."

"You're afraid we'll make fun of your dating moves, right?"

"Totally."

Ruby makes a weird sound, and I think she wants to laugh. "Crap. I need to get off the phone in a minute. Look, I know you're nervous, but think about how things went last time with Camden. You freaked and made a run for it. Doesn't it make sense to have someone around to give you a ride like at Hannah's party?"

"I guess, but promise you won't embarrass me. And no heckling."

"We'll do our best."

Though glad to have the backup, I'm more than a bit bothered I'll act dumber in front of Camden if I have an audience.

"Fine. I'll text you once he shows up after work and tells me where he wants to go. You know, assuming he actually shows up. If not, you need to pick me up."

"Done and done. I need to go."

Ruby hangs up before her boss catches her on her cell. I don't have to worry since my manager is outside arguing with someone on the phone. The laundromat is empty except for one regular, who spends most of his day watching the overhead TV. I suspect Barney has several safe, air-conditioned places to spend his days. He shows up here on Tuesdays and Thursdays. After smiling at him, I go about doing busy work.

By the time Andrea tells me she needs to run home to get something—which means she's meeting her boyfriend somewhere to continue their argument—I'm in full panic mode about seeing Camden later.

I end up thinking about the party when I enjoyed my first real conversation with him. Our circle of friends connected occasionally, and we'd shared a few passing hellos over the years. Ruby dated his cousin all through high school, so I knew the Rutgers without truly knowing them. That night at the party, I got to experience Camden very up close and personal.

Not wanting to attend Hannah's birthday bash alone, Harmony brought me along. She'd lost most of her friends when she had a kid, and they continued partying. Despite my aversion to being outgoing, I quickly transformed into a happy chick at the party. The music alone—an eclectic mix of the 1980s and 1990s alternative and pop music—put me in a great mood.

Suffering through one of her cleansing diets back then, Harmony couldn't drink alcohol.

"You should do a shot," she suggested, promising she'd keep an eye on me.

So I drank a shot of whiskey, which nearly made me puke. The screwdrivers were much better, and I downed two of them before Camden and Dayton arrived.

They were exceptional in a room full of average. I remember thinking they looked like Vikings ready to pillage our party. This image made me giggle. By the time I'd stopped laughing to myself, Camden stood at my side.

The party was too loud and crowded to hear most of what the sexy beast said. The only thing that mattered was how his warm, brown eyes focused on only me. I existed in a way I never did before or after that night.

The booze made me confident. When he kissed me by the fridge in the crowded kitchen, I hadn't pulled away. Instead, I threw myself at him, wanting more. I'd never been touched with such controlling care before.

In high school, a few boys kissed me, but they were sloppy and wore the bored expressions of guys willing to kiss anyone. Camden wasn't drunk or bored. He could have anyone at the party, but he was kissing me. And he was kissing me really fucking well!

Camden held me against his muscled body and sucked at my tongue as if in no hurry. I was comfortably against him and oblivious to the people around us. Camden's touch offered both heat and safety.

Wanting to be alone, we moved to a bathroom. Camden locked the door, and I stared at him like a dog in heat. If I had a tail, the damn thing would have been going a mile a minute.

A smiling Camden effortlessly lifted me up onto the counter, where his fingers explored the flesh peeking out from under my shirt. When his hand cupped my breast, I leaned into his touch. We existed outside of my typical worries. Right then, right there, I was a goddess, and he was my Viking.

Somehow, perfection went wrong. My panties were drenched, and Camden's skin was scorching under my fingertips. His shirt was off while my bra was pushed up. We were grooving until I panicked.

Outside of the bathroom, two girls screamed declarations of eternal friendship to each other. Their squeals startled my brain awake enough to worry about me naked in front of a damn mirror in a stranger's bathroom with a guy I lusted over but hadn't shared a real conversation with. *Was this really how I wanted to lose my virginity?*

More questions shocked me alert.

Did he have condoms? Was my untested birth control any good? What if I was bad at sex? What if I farted or made weird noises or looked stupid?

I mentally struggled with the many possibilities about what could go wrong. Then, Camden slid one of his big hands between my thighs, where I was hot and wet. Imagining how huge his dick likely was, I instantly feared I'd bleed to death from having sex.

A calamity of stupid is the only way to describe those next five minutes.

When I jerked away, the top of my head smacked into his chin. As he stepped back startled, I jumped off the counter with my usual lack of finesse. My hip nailed his erection straining against his tight jeans. Camden's pained grunt freaked me out even more.

I didn't know what to do. He frowned at me like I was crazy, and my mouth wouldn't work. *Had all the kissing broken my tongue?* Frozen in place, we stared at one another until Camden opened his mouth to speak, and I took off running. I don't even remember opening the door. I might have simply run straight through it like a cartoon character.

Finding Harmony dancing wildly in a crowd of people, I assumed she'd gotten drunk despite being the designated brain for the night. I barreled into her, still unable to speak. *What was wrong with my frigging mouth?*

My seemingly wasted sister proved to be bone-dry sober. Seeing me looking a mess, she never needed me to explain. She pulled me out of the house, only stopping at our car long enough to fix my bra and open the door for me.

We drove home with Harmony singing quietly with the radio. Nothing fazed her. She smiled even when angry. Meanwhile, I emotionally ran the gamut between drunken shaking and crying like a fool for embarrassing myself more than anyone had ever embarrassed themselves in the history of the entire frigging world.

"Did he hurt you?" she asked when we arrived at the trailer park.

Shaking my head, I regained the ability to form words. "I panicked."

"Who wouldn't? I'm sure it's a big dick," Harmony said and then climbed out of the car and helped my sloppy drunk ass into the trailer.

The next day, I woke up hoping everyone would forget all about my ridiculous behavior. Camden might call me an idiot, and people would laugh when they heard what happened. No biggie. Life would move on.

When Camden called my number, I refused to answer. His messages first asked and then demanded I call him, but I never did. How could I explain my freak out? I wasn't a teenager, and a grown woman should know how to keep her dignity intact in those situations.

After Camden labeled me a cock tease, guys pretended to be cold—shaking and chattering teeth kind of mocking—around me because I was so frigid. Girls joked they never had to worry about me stealing their men since I was all talk and no action.

Eventually, people lost interest and focused their teasing on someone else. By then, I'd already decided to lose weight and get my life organized. I planned to be healthy and smart. *Screw Camden Rutgers for destroying my confidence.* If our roles were reversed, I'd have pitied him for freaking out. Of course, the Rutgers family plays by a different set of rules.

Now Camden is back, claiming everything is cool, and we could pick up at the kissing part. My new insecurities and growling stomach say differently. There's no changing how I panicked and how he lashed out. Even if we both forgive and claim to forget, I plan to hold a grudge.

FIVE - CAMDEN

My fist barely makes contact with the guy's face before his nose explodes blood and teeth burst from his mouth. I step back and survey the damage. Behind me, a rested Dayton laughs like a hyena, and my father mutters something about my lack of control.

"Shit, boy, we don't want him dead," Mojo grumbles, standing next to me.

"It's not my fault his face is smaller than my fist. I barely touched the guy."

Mojo throws back his head and laughs. Violence makes him happy. I don't love it, but my size and power allow me to keep our family, club, and town safe. I do what I need to do, but sometimes things don't turn out how I plan.

My dad looks good for a middle-aged man with a rough life. His hair turned gray when I was a teenager but remains thick, while his brown eyes still sparkle when enjoying a solid beat down on a local thug.

"Good thing he's a pimp and not a ho, or you'd have killed his business," Mojo says, still grinning.

I kneel in front of the sobbing man. "You need to stop slapping your girls in public places in broad daylight. This is a family fucking town, and your shit ain't acceptable. Do we understand each other?"

The crying hustler nods and tries to stand, but pissing his pants seems to have turned his legs to mush. I suspect he'll crawl to safety after we leave.

"I wonder if his girls will respect him now," Dayton says as we stand outside the pimp's apartment complex.

"Probably not. Would you?" I mutter.

"No, but I've never been a whore paying sixty percent to a guy for protection."

"I always thought we should go into the prostitution racket," Mojo declares. "It's easy money to be made, and

25

we'd do better protecting the whores than the fuckwit inside."

Dayton and I share a smile. Mojo refuses to admit why we never added prostitution to the club's long list of criminal activities. We happen to know he made a promise to Grandma Rutgers years ago, and he couldn't break it without risking the curse she put on him if he dared go back on his word. Our grandmother was dead going on ten years, but Mojo still feared her wrath.

Women are tricky creatures, and even sweet girls like Daisy could hold grudges. I didn't mention my evening plans to my father. He'd think I'm an idiot. Rutgers men never chase women. They chase us.

Daisy is the exception. I fucked up by misreading her behavior that night, and a man needs to own his mistakes.

As soon as I split from Dayton and Mojo, I return my Harley to my condo. I shower, change my clothes, and decide to pick up Daisy in my black Escalade. After a frustrating stop at the flower shop, I arrive at the laundromat where Daisy finishes with work.

Her long brown hair is now shiny and straight, in stark contrast to when I found her waiting for the bus. No doubt she's cleaned herself up in preparation for our dinner.

"Good day at Suds N' Sun?" I ask when she appears outside.

"Yes, it was wonderful. Did you still want to talk, or can you just drive me home?"

I hand her the flowers, and Daisy looks at them confused. "They aren't daisies," I announce.

"I like daisies."

"Oh, well, I think there might be a few daisies in the mixed bouquet. The chick at the store said all of them had daisies in them. Did you want roses?"

"I'm not into flowers."

"Want me to throw them away?" I ask, reaching for the bouquet.

Daisy turns away, so I can't take them. "Nope."

"Let's go to the Boogie Bowl for dinner."

"Why?"

"Because I want ribs."

"Is there anything healthy there?"

"I don't know. But if what you want isn't on the menu, I'll ask them to make it special."

Daisy studies me with her hazel eyes, and I feel like a damn king under her gaze.

"You changed your clothes. Should I go home and change mine?"

I hear the challenge behind her question. If I take her home, I'll need to deal with the Lush Gardens family. She'll weasel out of dinner, and I'll end up playing twenty questions with Ruby or Harmony.

"You look gorgeous."

"You did, too. Why'd you change?" she asks, stepping back.

"I smelled from the heat, so I took a long shower."

Daisy's eyes switch from wariness to curiosity. I see her imagining me in the shower. Smiling, she shrugs.

"Thank you, I guess."

"You're welcome. Let's head out."

I open the door for Daisy, who climbs in and rests the flowers across her lap. By the time I reach my side, she's texting someone.

"Letting everyone know you're safe?" I ask, starting the SUV.

"Something like that."

Frowning at her, I settle back in my seat. "What happened to your job at the doctor's office?"

"They needed to cut staff, and I volunteered to go since everyone else has kids to support."

"You're a cool chick," I say, pulling into the afternoon traffic.

"This job is temporary until I improve my Spanish writing skills. There are a few jobs around here that I could get if I both spoke and wrote Spanish well. Right now, I'm only proficient in speaking."

"I thought you spoke French."

"I do."

"Damn, girl."

"Stop complimenting me so much."

Smirking, I pat her hand. "Baby, you get as feisty as you want, but I'm not good at taking orders."

"It feels like you're trying too hard."

"You make me nervous."

"Ditto."

"I always thought you were smoking hot, but I never saw a chance to make my move until Hannah's party. The problem was once I made my move, I kept on moving way too fast. Should have kissed you all over and then made plans for a date like tonight."

Daisy's delicate fingers caress the flower petals. She remains quiet while I deal with afternoon traffic. Hickory Creek Township isn't a big place, but the population grew fast, and the roads never caught up. With too many cars on too many two-lane roads, we take nearly a half hour to reach Boogie Bowl.

More than once during the drive, I consider asking questions to stir up a conversation. Except Daisy gives off an odd vibe, and I sense I should keep my mouth shut.

Before I can climb out of the SUV, she places her hand on my forearm.

"I'm sorry I freaked out and hurt you that night."

Our natural chemistry chips away at her pissed chick demeanor.

"I know, baby," I softly say, not wanting to rile her up again. "We managed to be at our best and worst that night. Let's try it again without the booze and rush to get naked."

Though Daisy nods, she exudes a depressed vibe. *Man, I sure have a helluva way with her.*

We walk inside, where I get us the best booth in the place. Daisy isn't the type of girl impressed by money, but I still want to show off for her. My inner caveman demands she knows I'm a good provider. To see Daisy smile, I'll get her the best booth, order any food she wants, kill potential predators, and buy her the best cave on the block.

SIX - DAISY

Camden smells fantastic, and I crave to lean closer to take a whiff. His shoulder-length blond mane remains damp at the ends. I remember how his hair felt against my fingers. I ought to hate a man having better hair than me. But with Camden, I always make exceptions.

"I have a confession," I tell him after a long, awkward silence at the restaurant table.

"Does it have anything to do with your sisters eating here?"

I glance at the doorway where Ruby and Harmony wave at me. "Yeah, I might have called them in as an exit strategy. Are you angry?"

"I'm never angry."

Though I want to roll my eyes, I don't. "Right."

"It's true. Nothing ever makes me angry."

"Oh, okay," I tease. "They're here as my backup, but now I feel guilty for asking them."

"Why guilty?"

"It seems insulting as if I'm saying you can't be trusted. Plus, now they have to eat at a restaurant pricier than we're used to."

"I'll pay for their meals."

"That's not necessary."

"I know," he says, leaning closer. "I am a very wise and gentle man. Now scoot off and tell your sisters I'm behaving well, and they can enjoy their dinners. Everything's on my dime."

"I don't feel comfortable with that."

"I know, but life is a complicated ride, and you need to choose the best exits."

"What?"

"Go tell them."

While I study Camden, my uncertainty only makes him smile wider. His lips curl upward in the most delicious way,

30

and I'm immediately overheated. Before he unleashes more of his manly magic on me, I slide out of the booth and walk to where my sisters sit with their kids.

"How's it going?" Harmony asks.

I've spent my life being the gawky middle sister. On one side, I have Harmony, who is a ray of sunshine on even the cloudiest day. Her golden hair comes from her Scandinavian father. Her tawny skin is from our mom's Greek side. Somehow, she manages to look both untouchable and like the girl next door.

On the other side of the spectrum, Ruby screams exotic beauty with her dark skin, eyes, and hair from her Jamaican-born father. She also possesses the tall, athletic build of our mother.

I manage to fall somewhere between Ruby's dark beauty and Harmony's light presence. I'm the product of Sally's attempt at a safe relationship. My father isn't sexy, and neither am I.

"What?" Harmony asks when I stare at her for too long.

"Nothing. I was just in my head."

"How's it going?" Ruby asks when I don't answer the original question.

"Fine. He's being sweet. He even said he'd pay for your dinner."

Ruby frowns, but Harmony's eyes light up. "Ooh, I want a burger, then."

"We don't want to owe the Rutgers anything," Ruby warns.

"No worries. Whatever we owe them, Daisy can pay off with her charms."

Though I open my mouth, my profane words die when I remember my niece and nephew are staring at me. Ruby's daughter, Chevelle, is curious about our discussion. She knows Camden better than we do, and I catch her waving at him.

Three-year-old Keanu only wants to color the kids' menu. He's mellow like his mom and completely disinterested in the drama around him.

"Don't be greedy with dinner," I warn my sisters. "I don't have enough charm for an expensive meal."

Harmony laughs. "Relax and enjoy the pretty man waiting for you."

"What she said, plus be careful," Ruby adds.

"I'm always careful."

My sisters share an eye roll and then focus on choosing their meals.

I hurry back to Camden, who smiles at my return. "Everything square?"

"Everything is perfect."

Camden gives me one of his sexy grins, and I nearly melt. Shaking off my dog-in-heat routine, I order fish and steamed broccoli while he wants half of the menu.

"I eat like every meal could be my last," he tells me.

"What else should I know about you?"

"What else do you want to know?"

"What's your favorite color?"

"White."

"I feel like you're messing with me."

"Can't a guy like white?"

"White is bland, and you're not a bland guy."

"What about you?" he asks while taking my puny hand in his big strong one.

"I like red."

"Fiery."

"Do you like being a twin?"

"It's good. I had a comfortable life, so everything was good. Now, if I were poor or short or fugly or whatever, maybe having to share the spotlight with another version of me would have sucked ass. For my life, it worked."

"Is Dayton your best friend?"

"I guess. I don't think about friends like that. I got my confidants, and that's Dayton and Bonn. Then, it branches out to my club brothers."

"Have you ever killed anyone?" I ask, wanting to get that right out in the open.

Without missing a beat, Camden shakes his head. "Of course not. Violence is wrong."

Fighting a grin, I ask, "Does your club do anything illegal?"

"No, we're mostly focused on fun runs. Lately, we've had a lot of pizza and painting parties."

Smiling now, I scoot closer to him. "I'm fairly sure you're lying."

"Why would I lie? I'm an honest guy. Ask anyone, and they'll say the same. Hell, they'll even say it with a smile on their face."

We share a knowing grin. "Oh, I bet they will."

"Have you ever broken any laws?" I ask, tapping my fingers against his brawny forearm.

"I admit, shamefully, of course, I might have jaywalked on occasion. And once I went ten miles over the speed limit, but I was in a hurry. I know that's no excuse."

"You're full of crap," I say, laughing. "You were speeding on the way here."

"Oops. I should work on that."

"Oops, my ass."

Even smiling, Camden gives me a wary look. "Do you really want to know where the bodies are buried, or would you rather remain blissfully unaware?"

This is how life works for those around the club. They know nothing. They accept everything. No questions. No expectations. Life is simpler that way, and Camden is asking if I can live blind to the club's business.

"Were you sad when your parents divorced?" I ask, changing the subject.

"No. I only want them to be happy."

"Who do you support in the election?"

33

"I wish everyone could win. Losing makes people sad."

Grinning again, I caress the rough hairs on his arm. "Do you have any regrets?"

"Just one. You."

My smile falters. "Why would you care that much about me instead of Ruby or Harmony or a million other girls?"

Camden studies me. "Tell me something. If I went to the restroom and Dayton came back dressed the same as me, would you be able to tell the difference?"

"Yes," I say immediately.

"How?"

"I don't know. He's different."

"We look the same. We sound the same. How do you know I'm not him right now?"

"It's something around the eyes," I say, caressing just above his right cheekbone. "Your smile is different, too, but I don't know how. It just is. The way you carry yourself is tighter than Dayton. Maybe in the shoulders. So, yeah, I can tell the difference."

"But none of those things would make you like me over him."

"No."

"Would you care if I left, and he spent the rest of our date with you?"

"Yes, because I like the way you look at me. Dayton looks at me differently. Besides, I don't want him to look at me the way you do."

"So, it has to be me?" When I nod, he smiles. "And that's why it has to be you and not your sisters or the millions of other girls."

I study him for a stupidly long time. "Can we have a real date?" I finally ask. "A real date where I'm not wearing 'geek' on my shirt and my sisters aren't keeping score. Is it too early to ask for another date, or do I need to wait to see if I ruin the rest of this one?"

"You think too much, Bourbon Babe."

"Is that a yes or no?"

Camden's large hand wraps behind my neck and guides me close enough for our lips to meet. His breath is hot, and he tastes like beer. I lean into the embrace, hungry for everything he offers.

Arriving with the appetizers, the waitress breaks up our kiss.

"That's a yes," he says and hands me a potato skin.

"I don't eat carbs."

"What the hell is a carb?"

"You know the answer."

Camden smirks. "Can tell when I'm lying, can you?"

"That time, I could."

"Look, I'm not a guy who bosses around his woman when it comes to what she eats. But just know if this no-carb crap is related to the rumor Brittany Sams started, you should dump your diet tonight. You were hot the night of Hannah's party, and you're hot now. Eat what you want based on what you want and not what that jealous bitch said."

I take the potato skin and set it on a small plate. "Brittany wasn't jealous of me."

"You can't be sure. Brittany has the stalker hots for Dayton and probably thought you were making out with him. Shitty stalker can't even tell us apart."

"I'm sorry," I tease. "Are you sad she isn't stalking you?"

Camden finishes chewing his potato skin and smirks. "I got plenty of stalkers."

"Name two."

"Jolene Baker from the Rite Aid and Louise Elson, who does my mom's hair."

"Jolene Baker is eighty."

"So?" he says, wrapping an arm around my shoulders. "Does she make you feel insecure?"

"She does have lovely hair."

"It's a wig. She threw it off once while chasing me through the parking lot."

35

I laugh because I think he's kidding. Camden gives me an odd look, and I realize maybe Jolene really did fly into an insane heat after seeing him one day.

"Were you hurt?" I ask, laughing.

"No, but she nearly clawed off my wife-beater."

"Well, if you were wearing a tight white tank, you really can't fault Jolene. I saw you wearing one of them while riding Shasta, and I nearly gave chase even though I hate running."

"You did, huh?" Camden says, tugging me closer. "I'll need to wear that on one of our dates."

The idea of having several more dates with this sexy beast sends me into confidence-overload. I lift my lips to his, and he devours my mouth in a wild kiss. If we weren't in public, I think I might have crawled into his lap. Knowing my family is nearby, I regain my senses.

"I'm not a brave person, but you make me wish I was," I murmur, fanning my cheeks.

"Courage is misunderstood. How do you know if you're brave until you've been in the position to decide between cowardice and courage?"

"I ran away the night of the party."

"That was all about emotion. Courage is about deciding based on logic to face something that might end badly. No emotion involved."

"Are you brave?"

"I'm willing to die and kill for what I believe in. I don't know if that makes me brave, but I know what matters."

"I'd like to think I'd do the same for those I love."

"You would. I can tell about people."

"I've never been a great judge of character. I see a smiling face and assume the person is harmless. On the other hand, I see a scary-looking person and think the worst, like with Melvin Shoals at Lush Gardens. He scared the shit out of me when I was younger. I hated passing his trailer and imagined him as everything from a serial killer to a monster of some sort just because he has buggy eyes and a scarred face. It turns out he's a super nice man. I can't trust my judgment with people."

"I know Melvin. He is a good guy," he says, studying me. "I sometimes wonder how you and I have lived in the same small town without crossing paths until recently."

"I wasn't ready," I say immediately. "I'm not sure I'm ready now, either."

"I'm a patient guy."

Nodding, I scoot over when our food arrives. I'm still hemming and hawing over whether to break my diet with the single potato skin. The last thing my willpower needs is for me to sit too close to his mounds of mashed potatoes.

Camden spends the meal giving me a load of lies about his club. *They organize food drives for homeless monkeys. His father reads to blind doves. His brother massages the feet of sad puppies.* So busy rolling my eyes and laughing, I barely obsess about how good his food smells and how much I want potatoes.

"Fish stinks weird," he says after we finish, and he stretches like he's making more space for his food.

Watching the muscles in his chest and arms flex, I feel like a shallow twit. Camden is more than his good looks. *But damn, does he have good looks!*

"On our next date, maybe you can try something that doesn't smell fishy," he says, cupping my face.

"Okay."

"You're fucking irresistible when you're stunned into mumbling."

Camden covers my mouth and kisses me so thoroughly I think I have a mini-orgasm. My panties, no doubt, need changing. As my mind swims, I realize I'd spend a lifetime doing nothing more than kissing this man.

The sudden burst of music pries us apart, but I can only admire the fierce man staring back at me. The intensity of his expression intimidates me, and the logical half of my brain warns I'm unprepared for Camden. Give me a decade with lesser men, and I just might have a shot at keeping up with this one.

"I don't know," I mumble, talking more to myself than Camden.

"Let's dance," he says.

The Boogie Bowl has a dance floor, and tonight's theme is the 1960s. I shake my head at the thought of dancing in front of the crowded restaurant. Camden stands up and tugs me to my feet. I tumble into him and hold on tight. My goal is to keep him from moving to the dance floor, but he easily maneuvers me to my terrifying fate.

"I can't dance."

"Everyone can dance. What you mean is you can't dance well," he says, blowing hair from my eyes as I stare up at him in horror. "I can't dance well either. Guess what? No one fucking cares."

I open my mouth to complain but then think of all the people staring at us. No way can they ignore Camden Rutgers on the dance floor. I feel their judgment without even looking around.

"Right here," he says, pointing his index and middle fingers at his face. "Look at me and don't look away."

I stare into his eyes and force a smile. As "Build Me Up Buttercup" begins to play, Camden takes my hands and forces me to sway with him. Whenever I think of looking around, Camden reminds me to focus on his face.

"I see myself as Fred Astaire even if I look like a dancing robot out here."

Laughing at his imagery, I relax as he spins us around the dance floor. I forget about the strangers watching us. By the next song, my sisters join us. Ruby and Chevelle display actual rhythm while Harmony and Keanu jump around to the music.

Reveling in this new confidence, I focus my gaze on Camden and shut out the world.

SEVEN - CAMDEN

I feel like a fucking stallion when I leave Daisy. My condo proves to be too small a stall, and I can't wait until I'm free of it. The next morning, I grab something to eat and drive around town. Twice, I pass Daisy's job and think of stopping. I need to taste her lips again. I want to taste more than that, too. After months of wondering and waiting, I'm dying to get shit moving.

Rather than showing up at Daisy's job, I head to the park next to my condo complex. Touch football sounds like a great way to work out my pent-up energy, and I pity the idiots standing in my way.

When I smash into him, Dayton goes down hard on the thick grass. I never hesitate on my way to the goal line. Throwing the ball on the ground, I wish I were pumping weights or running a marathon. Anything less can't calm me the fuck down.

"What in the hell did you eat for breakfast?" Dayton asks, standing up and shaking out his arms.

"What I always eat."

"Cold pizza shouldn't make you this hyper."

Hudson picks up the ball and throws a spiral pass to our cousin, Bonn. They don't seem interested in my drama, but Dayton's pissed.

"Hello? What's your fucking problem?"

"I have no problem. I'm just pumped."

"I guess Daisy liked her flowers," Hudson says nearby.

"Life is good, little brother," I announce and then look at Dayton. "Are we playing or what?"

"It's touch football, not tackle, fuckwit. Knock me down again, and I'll rip off one of your nads. Get it?"

"I hear your mouth flapping, but I don't see you making good on those threats, pretty boy."

Dayton rolls his eyes and gestures for Hudson to throw the ball to him. We return to the game, and I manage not to knock down my idiot brother. Hudson and I score a few times. Otherwise, we're crushed by Dayton and Bonn.

"The whole town heard about your horrible dancing," Dayton announces during our water break. "You sure know how to seduce the fucking ladies."

Ignoring his ribbing, I think back to how good Daisy felt in my arms. "She let loose on the dance floor. I fucking love when she laughs."

"Dude," Dayton mutters, shaking his head and giving me a weird frown. "Some things should be kept to yourself, and feelings are fucking one of them."

"Give him a break," Bonn says. "He's been circling that girl for a long damn time."

"That's fine. I'm all for him finally hitting what he's been hunting, but all the talk of feelings isn't cool. Dad says you should never shout your weaknesses unless you want your enemies taking advantage of them."

"I'm not shouting shit, and you aren't my enemy, cunt butler."

Bonn grins and smacks the side of Dayton's head. "You're such a daddy's boy."

"The man knows his shit."

"Sally Slater sure made some sexy daughters," I tell Bonn while ignoring my brother's distaste for the conversation.

Nodding, Bonn smiles, and I assume he's reminiscing about his old flame, Ruby.

"We're going out again tonight," I tell Bonn.

"You're giving away all your power, asshole," Dayton says. "Women need to know you have other options, or they turn bitch on you."

"Did Dad say that too?"

"Don't you listen to him?"

"Not always. I mean, the guy loves to hear himself speak."

"Pot meet kettle," Dayton says, stretching for a few women passing the park. Once they giggle and keep

40

walking, he focuses back on me. "I still think it's a mistake to make your feelings obvious. Women don't respond to weakness."

"What do you think, Hudson?"

My Zen brother ponders the question even though he's never had a girlfriend, let alone sex.

"I believe a girl will like a guy regardless of him sending her flowers or sharing his feelings. If she doesn't want him, he can do everything right, and she'll still think he's unworthy."

"The boy speaks the truth," Bonn says. "Remember Tim in high school? He had a thing for Jeannie, so he learned all he could about what she liked. He did everything right, and she still blew him off. Instead, she was hot for that jock she had nothing in common with. You can't force things. If it works, it works."

"Says the guy whose dick hasn't enjoyed pussy in years," Dayton grumbles.

"Classy," Hudson mutters, walking away with the ball.

"There's more to life than dick and pussy," Bonn tells Dayton.

"Yeah, like the club and our Harleys. Food's important, too. And beer."

"I'm over the pussy phase," I announce. "I want more, and Daisy offers it."

Dayton makes a gagging noise. "First, Ruby broke Bonn. Now, Daisy is snatching up your nuts. Where does that leave me?"

"Chasing Harmony," Bonn points out.

"I don't chase her. Do I see her and want to bend her over a table and fuck her? Sure. Would I like to have my dick in her pretty mouth on occasion? Yes. Does that mean I'll send her flowers and share my feelings with her? Not in a million fucking years."

"Harmony is just another chick to you. For me, Daisy is unique."

"Why?"

Both men stare at me, and I hate ending up on the damn spot. While I consider punching one of them to change the subject, I shove my hands into my pockets instead.

"When Daisy looks at me, I feel seen in a way I never do with other women. When I make her laugh, I feel like I've done something amazing."

"That's the stupidest shit I've ever heard."

"Fine. Daisy is beautiful, and she makes my dick hard, and I want to fuck her. But then after I fuck her, I still want to talk to her."

Dayton considers my words and walks away. "Whatever floats your boat, but you sound like a damn fool."

Next to me, Bonn wants to share his feelings on the matter. I suspect he won't speak up unless I beat it out of him.

"Spill it, cousin."

"I like Daisy, but I don't know if she has the stomach for your life."

"My life, huh?"

Bonn's a big guy, but he carries himself like an old man. I've always figured he wanted people to ignore him, so he works to disappear. Now, he puffs out his chest and shoulders, looking nearly as big as me.

"Don't play that game with me. We know the Brotherhood spills blood when necessary. Some women can handle that life. I don't think Daisy is one of them. She's fragile in too many ways."

"My business doesn't need to affect Daisy in any way."

"What about your dad? Or the club guys? Do you think Daisy will like spending time with them with the way they talk? Daisy isn't a wallflower. Not after living in Lush Gardens. She knows loud-mouthed people and booze-hounds and sluts. What she also knows is when violence breaks out, she should hide. She avoids danger while you seek it out."

"You're probably right," I mutter, running a hand over my sweaty forehead. "I'm not stupid or blind, but I won't walk away from Daisy now that I have a chance to see how things work out."

"I'm not telling you to do anything. I'm only warning you about problems that might come up. Despite what you think, you're naïve about shit, man."

"Naïve, my ass."

"Naïve is probably the wrong word," Bonn says, glancing around for the right one. "What you are is spoiled fucking rotten. You get what you want, and you think you'll always get what you want. The problem is sometimes things don't happen that way, and you're completely unprepared to zig if life zags."

"Yeah, like at Hannah Tripp's party."

"Exactly. You overreacted and fucked up things. I just don't want you doing that again since you seem to dig Daisy, and I know she's into you."

"She is, isn't she?" I say, grinning.

"She also went on a diet because she thought you called her chubby. You have the power to fuck her up, and I know you don't want to hurt her," Bonn says, pausing to frown at me. "If you do hurt her, you and I won't be so tight anymore."

"Because of Ruby?"

Bonn gives me a dark glare. "Because I have a daughter now. When I look at men like us with our bad behavior, I have no patience for it. You're smart enough and have a good enough heart not to hurt Daisy. So be careful. You don't need to end up with her, but don't treat her like shit because you get your precious spoiled feelings hurt."

"Solid deal. But when I lost my shit after the party, I didn't know her. I know her better now, and I'll keep my shit under control this time."

"Of course, you know her better. Months of stalking will do that."

"Fuck off, old man."

"What happens when she finds out you've scared away her potential boyfriends? Do you worry the stars in her eyes might dim?"

"Nope. She'll appreciate my commitment," I say, grinning while glancing at my approaching brother.

"Don't forget we have a work meeting tonight at the Corral," Dayton mutters. "I hate acting like your damn secretary."

"I'll be at the meeting, but I gotta leave in time to pick up Daisy. There's no fucking way I'll make a bad impression on our first real date."

"Asshole, the club comes first, and you'll stay as long as necessary. You know that." When I say nothing to Dayton, he adds, "Be there at three."

Gesturing a yes, I take the ball from Hudson and get in position. I'm uninterested in saying or doing anything that'll fuck up my good mood.

Daisy has something special going on, and I need to know if she can maneuver in my life. I won't let my jackass brother or anyone else get in my way.

EIGHT - DAISY

Men make a habit of standing me up on dates lately. The first time was a fluke. The third time was an insult. The sixth time was the final straw. While I have no idea what's wrong with me, men always find reasons to bail.

Now, Camden is late, and I worry he's suffering from the same buyer's remorse as my other no-shows.

Standing in the trailer park's west end parking lot, I fidget with my pink-and-black tie-dyed skirt again. For those first few minutes waiting for Camden, I'm the picture of confidence. The sexiest guy in Hickory Creek Township likes me. The night before, we kissed and danced. No matter what the future brings, I plan to have fun with him. No way will I ever have another chance with a man like Camden Rutgers.

As my confidence disappears, I wonder what in the crap I was thinking by picking a skirt to wear on a date with a biker. My black shirt is blazing hot from the sun, and my black knee-high socks are too loose and keep sliding down. I'm ready to retreat to my trailer where I can change and cry into a gallon of ice cream I know Ruby has stashed at her place. Before I can hide away, I spot Shasta racing around a corner and straight for me.

Camden's sexy Viking vibe is riding high tonight. His blond hair is wild from the wind, and his eyes shine with rage. I swear he's about to go into berserker mode.

"I'm late. I suck," he nearly shouts as soon as the Harley's engine goes quiet. "Business is my excuse. I will probably get my ass kicked for leaving early, but I'm here."

Camden sounds pissed, but I only stare at him in shock. I was so convinced he wouldn't show that I'm unable to accept this new reality.

"I like that shirt," I say when he scowls at me.

Glancing down at his plain white T-shirt, Camden grins. "I picked it just for you."

I smile since his teasing never feels mean. Stepping closer, I study the Harley.

"How come you call your bike, 'Shasta'?"

Camden shrugs. "Doesn't she look like a Shasta to you?"

Smiling, I have no answer since I've never met a Shasta before.

"How do I get on again?" I ask.

"I would have brought my SUV, but I was in a hurry to get to you."

"Of course, you were."

Camden only grins and helps me keep my balance as I climb on his Harley.

"I'm wearing shorts under my skirt. I don't know why I'm telling you that. I guess it's important for you to know I won't flash half the town during the drive."

Camden smiles at me over his broad shoulder. "You look gorgeous, but you already knew that."

"Oh, yeah," I say, rolling my eyes. "Let me get comfy here."

I wrap my arms around his hard, thick stomach. His muscles flex under my touch, and my body responds accordingly. If I could turn off my brain, I would fuck Camden right here in front of everyone. His body sings to mine, but my brain won't shut up.

As we speed down the road, I worry about falling off the Harley. I stress about looking stupid on the back of his Harley. I fear my hair will look crazy when we arrive. I worry about my breath, and if I'll have gas from my black bean salad at lunch, and if I'll say something stupid or will I say something really funny and give Camden the impression I'm funny when I'm certainly not.

I'm just completely frigging worried until I grind my teeth, and my palms sweat wildly.

"Chill," he says, glancing back at me when we arrive at Stella's Rib and Rub. "I know I'm an addictive beast, but put your vaginal needs in neutral until after dinner, babe."

I glare at him and then try to climb off. Remembering how I fell on my ass last time, I ease off the Harley but still lack my land legs and nearly topple. Camden wraps an arm around my waist and steadies me.

"You're so sexy when you do that," he murmurs.

I reach up to check my hair and wonder if I have a bug smashed on my face. Camden watches me checking myself, and I know he wants to laugh.

"You look like a mime doing that."

"I want to make sure I don't have anything stuck to my face."

"Huh?" he says, patting his cheek. "How about me? Did a bird take a dump on my noggin?"

"Funny."

"Are you okay?" he says, now touching my face. "Should I pat you down to be sure?"

Ignoring his offer to feel me up, I turn toward the restaurant. "This place doesn't serve anything healthy."

"I know. It's my favorite," he says, taking my hand and gently tugging me along.

We're seated in a choice spot by a very smiley waitress. I notice the way women look at Camden. They drink him in, and I want to do the same.

His wild hair gradually falls into a naturally perfect pose. His eyes no longer look angry. In fact, his entire expression is relaxed. Camden even smiles while looking over the menu.

"I'm still trying to eat healthy," I say once I realize my low-carb choices are nil.

"Take a vacation from that tonight."

"It'll go straight to my gut."

"Curves are hot, Daisy Bourbon Crest. Didn't you know that?"

I decide to pretend I'm a cool chick who eats like a man and never worries about getting fat. Is that the kind of woman Camden wants? I can do that even though I never ate the potato skin the night before. Yep, I'm a fearless eating

47

machine. You know, just until I've ordered my ribs and cheesy mashed potatoes. Suddenly, I'm hit with the reality of consuming thousands of calories and carbs.

"I can't do this," I say, resting my head on my arms and wishing to disappear.

"Eat a free meal with a sweet guy?"

Though I shoot him a dirty look about the "sweet guy" part, his smile tells me he refuses to be dissuaded.

"You're not a sweet guy, and I'm no free spirit."

"Okay."

Shaking my head, I want him to understand, even though I know he can't.

"The first time I saw you, I thought you were gorgeous." Hearing this, Camden smirks. "Everyone thinks you're gorgeous. Even lesbians do since they figure your long hair means you're a butch chick."

Camden considers this idea, decides it's a compliment, and then returns to smiling at me.

"So, when I saw you on your Harley, I imagined myself as a biker chick. I wore leather and a bandana like the girls who hang around your bar, Salty Peanuts. I pictured myself riding on the back of your Harley, and never once in my fantasies did I fall off and land on my ass."

"That's a sexy fantasy, babe."

"Ugh, you don't get it. That's what I do. When I was a kid, I wanted to be a ballerina. I imagined myself in my tights and tutu and dancing in front of an audience. Except I hate being on stage, I lack balance, and I have huge feet for my body. I'm an uncoordinated dolt, and no amount of dreaming would change how I'd never be a ballerina."

Camden watches me, but the effortlessly perfect man doesn't understand.

"Then, when I was in junior high, I dreamed I would be an athlete in high school. I wanted to be on the volleyball and basketball teams. I imagined wearing the uniforms and going on buses to games. I had it all planned in my head, even though I was still uncoordinated. Oh, and I hate sweating. There's sweating in sports, you know?"

"Yeah, I've heard that."

"You don't get it."

"What's wrong with enjoying a dream?"

"I build up fantasies in my head that I'll never accomplish. Like on my bucket list, I put I wanted to go cave diving in Vietnam and scuba diving in Belize. Those are stupid goals I can't accomplish because deep down inside, I don't want to. Hell, I'm too chickenshit to take a Caribbean cruise with my sisters."

"Who cares about caves and scuba crap? I know you want me to understand, but I don't get why you're upset."

"You're another unattainable fantasy like the basketball team and living in Japan for a year. I spend too much time in my head where I have dreams I don't want to make real. Do you get it now?"

"Why Japan?"

"Camden," I sigh when he refuses to focus.

He grins at my frustration. "I'm not like the basketball team or the other stuff. I'm sitting right here, and you like having me sit right here. This right now is real."

"The night of Hannah's party, I was acting like Harmony, not me. She told me to be her, so I did, and I had a great time. You and I had fun, and then I acted like myself, and you nearly lost a testicle."

"So, I'll learn to wear a cup around you," Camden says, wanting to laugh.

"You think I'm quirky or insecure by telling you this, but I'm being honest."

"No, you're trying to scare me away, but I fear nothing."

The urge to roll my eyes at his "fear nothing" declaration is strong, but I resist it. "I don't want to waste your time."

"Nope, babe. You're trying to avoid getting hurt."

"Okay, that, too."

"Well, since we're doing the honest route," he says, stretching his arms across the back of the booth.

Changing his posture makes him go from massive to super-duper-frigging-enormous. I'm a little afraid for my safety if he passes out, and I end up trapped under his giant body. On the other hand, of all the possible deaths I've feared over the years, this one sounds the sexiest.

"You're a dreamer, huh? Well, I'm a getter. In that, I get what I want. If I wanted to live in Japan, I'd move tomorrow. If I wanted to snorkel in Belize, I'd google Belize to find out where the hell that is. And if I want you, I'll stalk you and scare away assholes and wait until you're primed for the picking. Then, I'd swoop in and knock you off your fucking feet and make you mine. When I want something, I take it."

"Scare away assholes?"

"Just a few."

"Did you threaten them?" I ask, glaring at him.

"No, not really. Doesn't matter. They were wrong for you. I know what I'm doing even if you don't," he says, reaching for his beer. "And in case you're interested, I know you'd look fucking hot in a bandana."

"Actually, when I wear a bandana, I look like an old lady working in her garden."

"Not if the bandana is all you're wearing," he says, winking.

"How did you even know about my other dates?"

"Girls talk. You talked, and they talked, and I listened."

"Who are 'they' in this scenario?"

"If I tell you, you'll get mad at them."

"They're idiots who sold me out. Why shouldn't I get mad at them?"

"Good point. Well, the idiot you work with now plus Lindsey Buller from the trailer park."

"I never talk to Lindsey."

"Harmony does."

50

Frowning, I cross my arms and think of the nights I cried over being stood up. "Well, fuck you and them for ruining my dates."

"With the dental student who likes pigeons?" Camden asks, sounding as irritated as I feel. "Or how about the Italian taxi driver who was into boobs and said he would buy you new ones?"

"Those were two guys, and you're only picking out the ugly things about them. I could do the same with you."

"Doubtful."

"Your family business is—" Pausing to make him stew, I notice his expression turn grumpier. "It's complicated. Some women might have a problem with that fact about you."

"Some women don't mean shit to me. I'm looking at you, and I don't think you care one fucking bit about my complicated family business."

"Oh, I care."

Camden shakes his head. "Let's go back to talking about you wearing only a bandana. Feel free to imagine me only wearing a bandana, too, if it helps."

"Perhaps, that's why you want me. You need to get your fix. Like you need to know what you missed out on. Well, trust me when I say you missed out on absolutely nothing."

Camden gives me a dark frown, but I refuse to be intimidated. "After the party, I tried fucking a chick who looked like you, but I couldn't get into it. Then, I tried fucking a chick who was the complete opposite of you and—"

"Describe my complete opposite," I grumble.

"Blonde, super tanned, confident beyond human normalcy. She smelled like lemons, but she didn't interest me. I tried a redhead, too, but felt nothing. I went on dates with chicks, so I would look like I was dating and wasn't hung up on you. That worked until one girl thought I really liked her and got her feelings hurt when I didn't want a

51

second date. She fucking cried, and I have no tolerance for women crying. I mean, none. I can listen to a kid scream for hours without caring. But if a chick sniffles, I shit myself."

"When was the last time you got your jollies?"

"Jollies?" he asks, suddenly smiling. "Shit like that makes me dig you more. To answer your question, the last time was a few nights before you nailed me in the balls and took off running."

"I think you're lying."

"You're too cynical. Why would I lie?"

"I don't know," I say, shrugging. "Men lie."

"Women lie, too."

"Should we have sex to get it out of your system?"

"Do you want to have sex?" he asks and chuckles. "Of course, you do."

Narrowing my eyes, I mutter, "I'm not sure I want you to be my first lover."

"I like when you say 'lover.' It sounds possessive. I want you to grab onto me and just take what you want," he says, nearly laughing.

"Is your thing well-proportioned to the rest of you?"

"My thing? Oh, yeah, it's pretty large. I once nailed a divorcee who'd pounded out five kids, and she said I stretched her out good."

"You're gross."

Camden enjoys messing with me. I suspect my irritation at him scaring off my dates has set off his male anger.

"You asked about my thing's size. I was content keeping things PG-rated."

"Well, I'm not looking to bruise or tear, or whatever else can happen. I think I'll go with someone smaller for my first dozen times and then move to a larger size. Eventually, I'll work my way up to your massive thing, and we'll scratch that itch of yours."

"Bourbon Babe, if I wanted a bunch of dicks jacking you all up, I wouldn't have chased off all those turds."

"How exactly did you chase them off?"

Sliding closer as if sharing top-secret info, he softly says, "The key to lying is not telling the same lies too many times, or they take hold. That's why if I'd been the only one to call you a cock tease, it would have died off. Brittany Sams said it again and again with her dipshit friends, and it became fact."

"You're an asshole."

"Not as big an asshole as Brittany Sams. You should focus all your hate on her."

I smile despite my best efforts. "You're still an asshole."

"Sure, but I did you a favor with those guys."

"What did you tell them?"

"Well, different stuff. You don't want to know."

"Now, I do."

Camden glances around as if looking for help. I watch him and wait. Despite our food getting cold, I want to push him and see what hides underneath his cool exterior.

"You were my baby mama with one guy. I said you were a thief to another. A third might have heard you're a dude."

Sinking deep in the booth, I can't believe someone would think I was a man.

"I hate you," I mutter.

"Don't be like that. None of those guys were worth your time. You deserve a strong man with great teeth and his own place. Someone who brings flowers and takes you out to eat and convinces you to dance. Yeah, that kind of guy sounds great."

Camden grins, obviously quite satisfied with his efforts. I shake my head and try to get angry, but I hadn't wanted to date those guys. It still hurt getting stood up by so many of them. *What kind of loser was I if a loser didn't want to date me?*

Now I know the losers did want to date me. Not that my life is suddenly better from having this knowledge. However, my confidence definitely enjoys a shot of adrenaline.

"Why me?" I ask after too much time in my head.

Camden is halfway through his ribs when I speak up. "Oh, you're still talking to me? I wasn't sure since you were just sitting there."

"I'm a dreamer. I like being in my head. I told you that information less than ten minutes ago. You might have great teeth, but your listening skills need work."

Camden slides even closer. "I waited for you. Doesn't that count for anything?"

Fighting a smile, I shrug. "I guess. I mean, how hard could it be to wait for a few months?"

"So hard that I needed medical attention on several occasions."

"Why?"

"Oh, Bourbon Babe, are you so clueless about sex that you have to ask?"

"Yes."

"Wanked the dong too often."

"Eww," I say, laughing despite all the maturity in the world.

"Don't tell me you never masturbate."

"Not with a vibrator."

"Shit. Say that again but slower." When I only stare at him, he adds, "It's been a long few months."

"I use my hand like you do, but I've never injured myself. You must be weird or doing it wrong or probably weird."

Camden's gaze drinks me in, and I feel like the sexiest woman alive. "You could teach me a better way. I'm all about learning."

"I'll be horrible at sex. I just know it."

"I thought the same thing when I was young, but it turned out I was a natural. I bet you are, too."

"You're mocking me."

"Teasing you is all. Don't be sensitive."

"I'm always sensitive."

"Always?"

54

"Every waking moment."

"I like that. I'm never sensitive, so you always being sensitive would make us a good match."

"Is there anything I could say to scare you off like you scared off those guys?"

"Shit, I doubt learning you were sporting a dick would be enough to scare me off at this point."

Laughing, I scoot closer to him, and our hips touch. "I'm feeling brave. Won't last, so don't get too attached."

Camden shares my smile. "You're a fantasy come alive."

"I could say the same about you."

"That night at the party, you claim you were doing an impression of your sister. Does that mean you weren't speaking French? I don't know if I'd be able to tell either way."

"No, it was French."

Camden studies me intensely, and I can literally feel his temperature rising. "That was sexy as hell, and I don't know or like shit about France. I just know you sounded like music when you spoke in French while I kissed your neck. Do you remember that?"

"Yes."

"Can you say something in French now?"

I stare into his mahogany eyes and shiver at their warmth. Cupping his jaw, I wish he understood how we can live in the same town yet exist in different worlds.

"You're effortlessly beautiful," I murmur in French, and his smile grows. "No doubt, you wake up gorgeous. You're flawless even when you fail. You're brutally perfect even when you act like an idiot. How can I ever feel worthy of a man as bright and powerful as the sun?"

Camden doesn't understand my words, but he seems to sense the meaning behind them. His lips press gently against mine. He wants me to understand he feels my pain. When the kiss deepens, his hunger remains apparent. Despite my pain and fear, Camden gets what he wants, and he won't let anyone, including me, stand in his way.

NINE – CAMDEN

Ditching the club meeting early puts me in a world of trouble. I feel like a fucking asshole walking out when my father orders me to sit back down. Despite my oath to the club, I can't stand up Daisy. She's too damn sensitive for me to blow off. Especially after I convinced so many other men to walk away.

The look on her face when I arrive tells me she was minutes away from storming back to her trailer and calling me an asshole forever. Once she accepts I'm really in front of her, something staggeringly sexy clicks in her eyes. I'm back in her good graces, and she isn't only playing along as she was the night before. She's totally with me on this date, and I've got a real shot at fixing what I broke months ago.

Now we're at the restaurant, coming down from my admitting I've meddled in her romances. I feel no shame in lying to those guys. I'd have threatened them if I didn't think they'd end up whining to her. With the lies, they wanted away from Daisy rather than finding a way to weasel past me.

I might have forgotten to mention how I'd scared off men before Hannah's party. I've had my eye on Daisy for a while. What she doesn't know won't hurt her. Besides, she's calmed down enough to dig into the fattening food. Her expression is nearly orgasmic when she tries the mashed potatoes.

"That's my Bourbon Babe."

"Why do you keep calling me that?"

"Your middle name is Bourbon, and you're a babe. I thought that was obvious."

Smiling sweetly, Daisy is in a relaxed mood despite our earlier bitchiness. "I'm giving you a nickname, then. I was thinking Cheesestick, but that's too obvious."

Remaining silent while eating her food, Daisy struggles to pick a name that'll bug me. I don't care if she calls me

57

pussy willow. Watching her eat the mashed potatoes is worth whatever teasing she attempts.

"I can't think of one."

"My mom calls me Cami. Dayton calls me BO. As you can see, I'm used to less than manly nicknames."

"Everyone calls me Daisy."

"I'm not everyone," I say, winking at her. "I never have been, and I don't see the point in starting now."

"What's it like to be different from everyone else?"

"It's fucking fantastic." Daisy nearly laughs at my statement, but I don't think she can see me past the food on her plate. "When was the last time you got naughty with your food choices?"

"Naughty?"

"You look guilty."

"Well, it's super fattening."

"But it's good, right?"

"It's fucking fantastic."

We share a smile before she returns to eating. I find her sexier with every bite. She's embracing a bad choice, and I want her to dive headfirst into a relationship with me. I might be a handsome guy with cash in his pocket, but I come with a minefield of problems a good woman won't want to step in. If Daisy's going to give in to the idea of us, I need her to find me as irresistible as those mashed potatoes.

"I missed carbs," she says, leaning back and patting her stomach.

"Before that night, you ate like a normal person, right?"

"Normal person?"

"Like your sisters, I guess."

"Yeah," she says, looking edgy.

"And you stopped because of the rumor started by Brittany Sams?"

Daisy opens her mouth to correct me on how the rumor started, but she changes her mind and only nods.

"Now, we're starting over, so that rumor never happened. I assume that means you can enjoy carbs again."

"Do you not like the way I look now?" she asks, crossing her arms in the classic pissed girl stance.

"I already said you're gorgeous now, and you were gorgeous the night of the party. No way will you get me to say otherwise."

Daisy startles me with her sudden grin. "You look afraid."

"I want things to be solid between us."

"I'm here pigging out on potatoes and thinking about what you taste like. I'd say things are solid."

My lips are instantly on hers, and she laughs until I steal her breath. I like the way she moans and leans into my embrace. No longer playing shy, Daisy's in it to win it.

A loud laugh at a nearby table startles us apart, and Daisy glances around as if suddenly remembering we're in public.

"You make me…" she trails off rather than finishing.

"Yeah, you make me, too."

Daisy studies my face. "Does nothing really scare you?"

"Not a damn thing," I say, though I was fairly scared about ruining our date, and I'm not really looking forward to the beat down I have coming later.

Daisy's smile widens. "Everything scares me."

"No, I don't think so. You didn't seem scared standing at the bus stop with those guys nearby. You didn't seem scared the night at the party. You didn't even seem scared when you thought I stood you up. I don't think you're nearly as scared as you are stuck on what others do. Just because you don't like something doesn't mean you're a chickenshit. A lot of people like the idea of traveling but don't want to travel. They're not scared, and I don't think you are, either."

Daisy considers my words. "I am scared of looking stupid or failing."

"That I believe."

"I'm not scared of you, but I'm afraid of your opinion of me. Does that make sense?"

"Yeah, but my opinion is all happiness and joy, babe."

"I'm sorry for all this talk about feelings and fears. Lame date chatter, I know."

"It's all good. You've spent months thinking I'm an asshole when I'm really the nicest guy in the world."

Daisy shakes her head. "None of the women in my family have great luck with men. Mom had three kids with three men. Harmony has odd taste in guys. Of course, Ruby was screwed by Bonn. It's made me overly jaded when I should be only regular jaded."

Hearing Bonn's name makes me tense. I know his history with Ruby and why Daisy thinks he's a jerk. It all makes sense in my head, but I still open my mouth and start shit.

"Bonn is a good guy."

"If you say so," she immediately replies, and her body goes stiff next to mine.

"Bonn loves his kid."

"I never said he didn't."

"A lot of women think a man who's bad at relationships can't be a good father."

"I'm not a lot of women. I'm me, and I never said that."

"But you hold a grudge against him."

"Not because I think he isn't a great father."

Feeling grumpy, I think of how many nights Bonn and I sat on the roof of our condo complex. He never got over Ruby, but he's still a bad guy in the eyes of too many people. "It was a long time ago."

"He broke Ruby's heart. I know a lot of women can get over that, but Ruby isn't a lot of women, either. She loved and trusted him."

Rather than change the subject, I double down. "He was a young guy with a lot of pressure on him, and he made a mistake."

Daisy also refuses to back down. "Ruby was a young woman and pregnant with his kid. She couldn't walk away from the pressure. If he didn't want her, he could have ended things. Yes, she would have been upset, but she would have

60

eventually understood. Instead, he said he loved her and then fucked someone else. So, no offense, but who gives a shit about Bonn's pressure."

"He's always had it hard being on the outside."

"Ruby was good to him. She didn't put him on the outside."

"She got pregnant when they were barely out of high school."

"His dick got her pregnant."

"She said she was on the pill."

"She was."

Waving my hand dismissively, I resent how she won't give in to me like most people do. "He was overwhelmed."

"So was she."

"Well, he did his best, and he fucked up, and she should get over it."

"You should fucking get over it," Daisy grumbles, standing up and grabbing her purse. "I'm going home."

"You're losing your shit because I won't agree that Bonn is an asshole?"

"I never said he was. I said he broke my sister's heart, and she shouldn't have to get over that."

"They share a kid, so she should be smarter about shit."

"You mean, smart like when he fucked some chick and then came home to Ruby? What if he caught some disease and gave it to her and Chevelle? Ugh, forget it. I'm leaving."

I watch Daisy hurry out of the restaurant. A part of me considers letting her work out her anger a little before I follow. But she looks so damn sexy stomping out of the front door.

Daisy is already on the phone with Harmony when I reach over her shoulder and snag the cell.

"Hey, little sister, things are fine," I tell Harmony. "Camden will bring me home later. Don't wait up. Thanks, babe."

"What the hell?" Daisy cries, reaching for her phone after I hang up.

"You sure like to run away when shit ain't going your way."

Daisy glares ferociously at me, but I only smile. She's a fucking Amazon princess in her delicate little way, and it's making my cock rock hard.

"Look, you've got your sister's back. I like that you're loyal. I'm loyal, too. Bonn is my friend, and he's family. I don't care if he's wrong or right. I only know if someone talks shit about him, I'm going to defend him."

"Well, I'm going to defend my sister," she says and then adds quietly, "Especially when she's right."

"You don't like me taking his side, but you should appreciate how I'm loyal. That's a good quality, right?"

Getting my point, she grudgingly smiles. "Yeah, it's a great quality. Maybe you should teach Bonn about it."

"His dick has remained solidly in his pants all these years. That's a long time for a man. In fact, I read somewhere it's medically dangerous to go that long without sex."

"You read that, huh?" she asks and laughs. "Where?"

"Some porn site, I think."

As we both laugh, I step closer and wrap an arm around her shoulders. "It's dangerous for a man's heart not to have sex regularly. I think it's bad for his dick, too. But I didn't read that far."

"I love my sister," she says, relaxing in my embrace. "I saw how Bonn hurt her."

"Yeah, and I saw how Bonn reacted to losing her. It might be his fault, but I gotta take my man's side. It's just who I am."

"And this is who I am."

"I like who you are."

Daisy smiles up at me. "I'm a fan of who you are, too."

"So, let's go back inside and not talk about broken hearts," I say, nudging her toward the front door. "They have great apple pie, and I need a whole lot of sugar since I'm going home without getting laid again."

"What makes you think you won't get lucky tonight?" she asks, walking with me to our booth. "Is it because I lost my shit and ran away?"

"No, I want to take this slowly to show you that my interest isn't residual horniness from that night."

"But you are horny from that night. I am, too. It was a hot night."

Sliding in next to Daisy, I quickly kiss her. "Yes, it was, but I'm not a horny guy looking to scratch an itch. I dig this thing between us, so stop running away. Especially after I just ate, and my food is still settling. You don't want me cramping up."

Daisy pats my stomach and smiles for me. Soon, our pie arrives, and we dig in. Well, I eat most of it while she watches and talks about her favorite foods. They're all fattening shit I love. Her eyes light up when she describes her beloved burgers, making me especially hard. From now on, I decide to wear boxers on our dates.

Surviving climbing on and off the Harley without injuring herself, Daisy beams at me as we walk to her trailer. I'm on guard for her mom or sisters. We arrive without anyone showing up, but I feel the entire trailer park spying on us.

"Tomorrow, I'll come here for dinner," I say, wrapping her against me. "You can cook anything you want." Seeing Daisy's eyes widen in panic, I add, "Never mind. I'll surprise you with takeout at seven. I want to meet your cats and see where you hang out. We'll fool around on your couch, and I'll leave with a raging hard-on, and you'll be rightfully impressed by my self-control."

Daisy smiles so widely I bet her face will hurt later. "You have it all planned out."

"Every night since the party, I've been planning for this day, Bourbon Babe. You just relax and let me do the thinking."

Kissing her, I want to swallow this sexy chick whole. She tastes like barbecue sauce and a hint of apple pie. I know

I could carry her into the trailer, and she wouldn't refuse me. We're both curious as hell to see where our kissing could lead, but I grudgingly step back.

"Tomorrow at seven," I say and take another backward step. "Now, you better run and tell Harmony all the details of our big date. I'm sure she's curious."

Daisy gestures to the nearby trailer, where her sisters stare at us from the window. I wave at them, and they wave back. *Nothing at all awkward about having an audience.*

I leave Daisy, who watches me walk away. Before I disappear into the parking lot, I glance back and find her still smiling at me. She looks irresistible, and I know my impressive self-control won't hold out for too much longer.

Firing up the Harley, I finally check my phone and see a long list of furious messages from Dad and Dayton. I text to say I can meet them now and instantly receive a message from my brother telling me where to go. Retribution is coming. But with Daisy's flavor on my lips, the punishment will be worth it.

TEN - DAISY

As soon as Camden disappears into the night, I run to my mother's trailer, where my sisters still peer out at me. Sally's dark hair is wrapped in a messy bun on her head as she tosses a bag of popcorn into the microwave. My sisters sport unkept ponytails. I feel extremely sexy in comparison with my windblown hair from riding on the Harley.

"Have fun?" Ruby asks, joining Chevelle on the couch in the doublewide trailer.

With my lips still warm from his kisses, I smile. "I had an amazing time. Camden even convinced me to eat ribs and mashed potatoes. I haven't been this full in months."

"Bad men are bad influences," Harmony says, patting my stomach before joining Sally in the kitchen. "That's why I like them."

"He's coming over tomorrow for dinner."

"Can we spy?" Harmony asks.

"It might get PG-rated, so no."

"PG-rated," Chevelle says, looking at her mom. "I can watch that."

"Sometimes in movies," Ruby replies. "But never when Daisy does it. *Never.*"

Carrying a big bowl of buttered popcorn, Harmony walks back to the couch.

"Where's Keanu?" I ask my sister.

"Asleep in my trailer. Betty's watching him while we gossip. So, are you pregnant yet?"

"PG-rated doesn't allow for that. Besides, I'm on birth control."

Harmony and Ruby laugh, and I catch my mom smiling. "So were we," Harmony teases. "Use super strength condoms."

Ruby throws popcorn at our sister. "Let's keep the gossip from turning PG-13 rated."

"Message received," Harmony says, taking the popcorn from her hair and tossing it into her mouth.

When I catch Sally watching us, my gut twists. My mother's face shines even when she's enraged. The only time she doesn't glow is when she has bad news.

"You didn't ask my opinion," she says, and everyone's smiles fade, "but I'll give it to you anyhow. Dating Camden Rutgers is a mistake. Even if he's good to you, he isn't a good man. His family is tied to various criminal activities. He could end up in jail or dead. He'll likely cheat on you once your newness wears off. If you have his kids, he'll want them to live his miserable criminal lifestyle."

Even shocked by her harsh truth, I manage to blurt out, "I don't care."

"You should care. He's willing to ruin your life."

I look at my sisters for support but find them staring awkwardly at the ground. Focusing back on my mom, I shrug.

"I don't care what anyone thinks. Camden makes me feel great, and I'm giving him a chance. All that crap you said doesn't matter."

"That's my girl!" Sally declares, pulling me into a hug. "Don't let people and their opinions stop you from living."

"So, that was a test?"

"Your father will likely say the same thing when he hears about you and Camden, but I don't think you're interested in living Ollie's safe life. You want more, don't you?"

"I want Camden."

"He seems to want you, too. That's all that matters. Not anyone's expectations. Not tomorrow. Nothing. Just follow your heart. You're strong enough to handle the consequences."

Sally's meaning might be encouraging, but her words leave me nervous. I know she wishes I was carefree. I want to be that way, too. I've imagined myself being like her or Harmony, but I can't muster up the courage to follow their lead. My brain always gets wound up on the little details, and it'll no doubt happen again with Camden. Until then, I want to enjoy feeling beautiful with my Viking.

ELEVEN - CAMDEN

My uncle Jude Hallstead meets me at the door of the old hardware store we use for interrogations and beat downs. Howler is the Brotherhood's VP and my dad's best friend growing up. They came from opposite sides of the town's wealth divide but somehow ended up running a criminal organization together. A lot of men might have been pissed when their best friend cheated on their sister but not Howler. He's the biggest tang magnet I know, and Bonn isn't his only illegitimate kid running around the world.

"Your dick needs to stop running the show," Howler tells me as I enter the building.

Ignoring him and his bushy blond hair, I smile at Mojo and Dayton, along with a handful of other club brothers.

"Ain't it a wonderful day in the shits, gentlemen?" I announce. "Do your worst."

"What if I shot you, son?" Mojo asks, trying to seem taller than me. "Would your little girlfriend be worth taking a bullet to the head?"

"Hell, if ditching a meeting is all it takes to have you shoot me in the head, I'd say we might as well get it the fuck over."

Dayton stands behind our father, dismissively shaking his head.

"The club always comes first," Mojo says. "Before girlfriends. Before friends. Even before family."

"Thanks, Dad," I say, emphasizing the last word.

"You knew what you signed on for."

"If you want to make an example of me," I say, tossing aside my jacket and stretching out my arms, "let's do this. But I didn't sign on to be your bitch. I'm Camden Rutgers. I do what I want. Now, let's get this done."

The first hit is always the worst. Once the pain kicks in, the adrenaline does, too. Instantly, I feel invincible.

Dayton barrels into me, going low like a linebacker before using his shoulder to nail me in the ribcage. I grunt before swinging to the side and sending him toppling. While I might accept a beating for my transgression, I won't play the martyr. If they want to punish me, they'll need to embrace the pain, too.

Mojo and Howler double team me. Dad hits me in the jaw while my uncle's punch makes contact with my ear. Despite seeing stars, I play The Three Stooges by grabbing them by the hair and slamming their heads together.

Outnumbered, I can't avoid getting pummeled, but I make every guy earn each punch and kick. My club brothers want me to know my place, and I expect them to understand the same. One day, Mojo will retire, and I plan to lead these men. I won't take shit from them now, and I won't do it when they call me president.

"Good boy," Mojo says after the beating is over, and he's nursing his wounds. "Next time, make your pussy wait."

"No," I tell him, walking away. "I'm hardheaded, Dad. You ought to know that, especially after my noggin nearly broke your jaw."

Mojo shoots me a dirty look, but I'm already on my way outside. I refuse to show pain. I won't even limp despite my right knee throbbing from Dayton's righteous kick.

As everyone else goes their separate ways, I feel my brother following me. I stop at my Harley and spit out a gob of blood.

"You hit like a fucking pansy, Daycum," I say, grinning at him.

"I can't believe you went for my balls. That's a chick move, Cumdud."

Smiling, I cross my arms and then remember my bruised ribcage. Uncrossing them, I'm careful not to reveal my pain.

"Sissy," Dayton says, knowing me too well. He studies me with eyes I see every damn time I look in the mirror. "You've built up this chick too much."

"Fuck that. I'm doing what we always do. I saw what I wanted and took it."

"Do you know why I chase Harmony and never catch her?"

"Because she won't let you."

"Fuck that. I'd catch her if I wanted to, but I never will because the reality of Harmony can't live up to the fantasy. So, what happens when the reality of Daisy can't live up to whatever you've created in your fat head? Once you've gotten in her bed and she's no longer the forbidden fruit or prize, what then? What happens when she's just an ordinary chick sitting there expecting shit from you? I'll tell you what happens. You'll dump her or stick around unhappy until she dumps you."

"Bullshit."

Dayton pokes me hard in the chest. "You see yourself as a nice guy, but you're making Daisy promises you won't keep. You think Dad is a loser with women, but he knows he's no good with them. So, he fucks stupid sluts who don't expect anything. Any decent woman deserves more than he can give. That's why he doesn't mess with them since Mom. You should learn from him."

"I am learning from him."

"How the fuck do you figure that?" Dayton nearly yells.

"He had his perfect woman with Mom, but he got bored. Instead of finding ways to make their life better and more exciting, he fucked someone else. Since then, he's fucked plenty of other women, but he'll never find another woman like Mom."

I pause to spit out more blood and run my tongue over my teeth to make sure they're all intact.

"One day, he'll be old as fuck, and twenty-year-old sluts will suck him off and giggle at his stupid jokes. Except they'll only do it if he still has power and money. If he gets hurt or ends up broke, do you think any of those girls will waste their time with him? Do you think they'll take care of him when he's sick? Nope. He's only as sexy as his power

70

and money remain attractive. In reality, he's a lonely, old man begging for scraps from bimbos. I won't follow that fucking route."

"So, you think you can force something with Daisy?" Dayton mutters and then adds, "Mom turned out fine."

"Yeah, she did because she didn't spend the last twenty years fucking random people. She found an imperfect man and focused on what was great about him. Mom stayed with Erik like she would have stayed with Dad if he hadn't fucked half of her friends."

"You've got stars in your eyes, man. It's scary."

Leaning against the Harley, I sigh. "I like the way Daisy makes me feel. No other chick does the same to me. So, I'm making the decision to go all-in with her. I won't be a coward fearing a bad end like you. You're fearless in a fight. But with a woman, you want to play shit safe. Think about that, man."

"Don't call me 'man,' or I'll knock you so ugly people will finally be able to tell us apart."

"Oh, don't you worry about people telling us apart. One day, I'll be the guy with a wife and kids, and you'll be the old perv picking up nineteen-year-olds for sloppy blowjobs behind a dumpster."

My brother says nothing, but I doubt my words have turned him wise about relationships. Tonight, he'll likely hit a bar and hook up with one of those nineteen-year-olds for a quickie. While he races off to another meaningless night with women who can't tell us apart, I only have one woman in my sights.

And nothing anyone says will change my mind.

TWELVE - DAISY

Camden calls me at work to say he can't make our date. I worry when he claims he's sick because I know that's man-code for injured. Camden laughs off my concern and promises he'll bring me the best damn takeout Tennessee has to offer.

Left without a date, I hang at home with my family on one of the best days of the week. Wednesday nights mean drinks, poker, and ribbing at Lush Gardens. Sally and her best friends, Betty and Charlie, started the tradition when Harmony was a newborn. Since going out to party was no longer an option with three little ones at home and dealing with her postpartum funk, the ladies decided to bring the fun to the park.

A few folding tables were set out between the trailers. Chips, salsa, and mojitos were served while the women played cards. I remember sitting in the trailer, peeking out at my mom laughing her ass off with her friends. Playing cards looked to be the most exciting thing ever. Later, I realized poker, booze, or snacks didn't make the nights fun. It was about surrounding themselves with people who loved and appreciated them.

I never found that kind of acceptance from school friends while my trailer park friends moved on with their lives as soon as they hit eighteen. The only girls I ever got along with completely were my lovably annoying sisters. We eventually joined the card games. Even though Ruby has never won a single hand, and Harmony refuses to remember which card combinations are better than others. I take poker more seriously, only because I tend to take most things too seriously.

Pigging out on nachos and guacamole, I know I need to slow down on my calorie intake, but carbs are so damn good. Now that I've indulged in them again, I refuse to stop. I wonder if sex with Camden will have the same effect on me.

"I better get the sex done before I gain eighty pounds," I announce. "On the other hand, I'm scared poop-less of sex with a giant man. Can it injure me?"

"Most definitely, but it'll heal," Betty says.

Grimacing, I look down at my crotch. "Anything I can do to prepare for it? You know, like exercises or breathing techniques."

Their laughter pisses me off, but my anger only entertains them more.

Harmony leans her head on my shoulder. "If you get lubed up really nice beforehand, you should be fine."

"So, buy some lubricant? Check."

"No, baby," Sally says, chuckling at my stupidity. "You gotta get him to lube you up with foreplay."

"Is that something I ask for, or will he know to do that?"

"A man with Camden's experience ought to know, but men are often lazy," Sally says, shuffling the deck.

Ruby sits on my other side and hands me a mojito. "Keep your legs closed while making out. Make him work to get them open by giving you lots of foreplay. Don't just let him rip off your panties and go to town."

"Ugh. I think I'll stay a virgin."

"Look, I won't lie," Sally says, taking a puff from her cigarette. "It'll probably suck pretty hard the first time around, even if Camden has mad skills. Fucking is a two-person activity, and you don't know what the hell you're doing. I suggest you accept it'll be bad, but plan to get that first time out of the way and enjoy the second, third, fourth... Well, you get the picture."

"With Camden having so much experience, should I check to see if he's tested for diseases? Is that something I can ask?"

"You can ask anything you want. There are no rules in life."

Rolling my eyes, I can easily list ten life rules just off the top of my head. Ruby takes her cards and looks them over.

"My first time was great because I was with someone I loved, not because it was any good physically. Neither Bonn nor I knew what we were doing. If you're into Camden, the sex will be great because it's him, even if you fumble around."

"What if I injure him?"

I know before I finish the question that I've opened myself up to laughter. They enjoy a good chuckle at my expense.

"It'll be okay," Harmony says, giving me a supportive grin. "You always overthink things that don't need much thought. Just tell Camden you're nervous and don't know what to do and let him lead. Just like he led when you were dancing at the Boogie Bowl."

Ignoring the cards in my hand, I think of Camden holding my hands and guiding me. Our dancing wasn't sleek or sexy. We were having fun, and the world disappeared around us. I only saw him, and I do love that view.

THIRTEEN - CAMDEN

Breaking my date with Daisy nearly kills me, but I don't want her seeing me fucked up. My eyes and lips are swollen. My knee is sore and stiff. My bruised ribs make breathing painful. I'd still drive over to see her if my only concern was the pain. A man can swallow a whole lot of suffering when a beautiful girl is involved.

If Daisy sees my bruises, she'll freak the fuck out. The girl's no fighter, and I doubt she's suffered a single black eye in her entire life. Violence to Daisy is ugly and unacceptable. How can she understand I agreed to the beat down to be with her and protect my reputation?

Pacing around my condo, I need to keep my distance from Daisy for a few days. I should play things cool, and I'm an ace at self-control.

Knowing shit and actually doing shit are two very different fucking things, and I find myself riding Shasta to the Lush Gardens Trailer Park just after eight in the evening.

I walk from the parking lot past several trailers where the occupants quietly watch TV. Closer to Daisy's place, I hear music playing and women's laughter. Before revealing myself, I catch sight of a group of people in the lane between Daisy and her sisters' trailers.

"Mustang Sally" and her best friend "Black Betty" are having a dance-off to "Play That Funky Music." Harmony holds Keanu in her lap while they clap along. I notice Ruby carrying a big bowl of chips to the table. Chevelle is right behind her with what is likely dip. At the table sits Billy, the trailer park's manager, and his wife and the third of Sally's crew, Charlie, a.k.a. "Charlotte is a Harlot." The entire family is present except for my girl, instantly putting me on edge.

"This is why I'm glad I never had sons," Sally announces while still dancing as I approach them. "Look at what someone did to this boy's handsome mug."

Betty claps her hands to the beat. "Rutgers boys can take it, right, Cam?"

I don't know these women any more than they know me, but in Hickory Creek Township, no one's business is really private.

"You should see the other guys," I say, giving them a smile even though it hurts to move my face.

"No doubt," Sally tells me before walking back to the table and lighting a cigarette. When she notices me watching her, she smiles. "Do you know what the secret is for handling bad habits?"

I shrug, and Betty laughs. "It's all about knowing your boundaries."

Sally winks at her friend. "We only smoke when we drink, and we only drink when we gamble, and we only gamble with people we trust. That's how we keep it safe and sane."

A curious Chevelle walks over to me. She's a tall kid with big brown eyes and a lopsided smile. I see both Bonn and Ruby in her. But right now, she reminds me of her aunt.

"Does it hurt?" Chevelle asks.

I squat down, so we're at eye level. "Naw. Looks worse than it feels."

"Are you here to see Daisy?"

"Yep. Is she around?"

"Her cats were fighting, so she went inside to dope them up with catnip."

Grinning, I glance at Daisy's trailer, where Harmony stands at the doorway. I wait to see the face I can't get out of my mind. Daisy pops her head out and stares at me. I see the horror in her hazel eyes even from this distance.

Daisy hurries to me and reaches to touch my face. Changing her mind, she pulls back her hands.

"What happened?"

"I had to put some people in their place."

A hint of a smile touches her face and then is gone. "Are you okay?"

"Sure."

Daisy hears something in my voice because her concerned expression shifts, and she rolls her eyes.

"Male bravado," she mumbles, turning to look at her family now playing cards. "I'm ditching you again."

"Be sweet to the boy," Betty says, shuffling cards. "He's had a rough day."

I hear the women and Billy chuckling. In their minds, violence is part of who I am. I doubt Daisy feels the same way.

Taking my hand, she leads me to her trailer. I walk inside and inhale her fruity scent lingering in the air. I've been curious about Daisy's place for months. I glance around and take in everything I can.

Daisy sure digs patterns and not only on her outfits. I notice a rug with brightly colored spots on the living room floor. Her table lamps are black and white striped, while her dark couch is covered with polka-dotted throw pillows. One wall in her small kitchen is painted bright pink. Another is pale blue with pink circles and swirls. There's no doubting the trailer belongs to Daisy Bourbon Crest.

"What happened for real?" Daisy asks, letting go of my hand and walking to her small kitchenette.

I realize what her distance means. If I tell the truth, she'll let me get close. If I lie, well, I'm on my fucking own.

"This is my punishment for ditching a club meeting."

Daisy stares at her hands, and I know she's wondering the same thing I am. *Can she live the club life?*

"Which cat is this?" I ask, glancing down at the black-and-white creature rubbing itself against my leg.

"Seoul."

"Like heart and soul?"

"No, like the South Korean capital. I'm trying to learn the language, but I couldn't get Chinese and Japanese right."

"Why?" I ask, leaning down to pet the cat that seems hotter for me than its owner.

77

"They're hard languages," she says like I'm an idiot. "Spanish, French, English have common sounds and words, but Asian languages are entirely different beasts. Harmony and I are learning Korean together, so I don't plan to give up this time."

"For Keanu?"

Daisy nods, and I think about her half-Korean nephew. He's a cute kid with his dad's coloring and Harmony's facial features. Keanu owns his mom's smile.

"I like your place," I say like a fucking dweeb. When I stretch slightly, my hands scrape the low ceiling. "But I'm sitting down."

Walking to the couch, I kick off my shoes and get comfortable. If Daisy wants me out of her trailer, I don't plan to make it easy for her.

"Do they have Korean names, too?" I ask, gesturing to the two cats sitting on the back of the couch.

"No. One is Hong Kong, and the other is Tokyo. They're Seoul's sons."

"How did you end up with three?"

Daisy watches me from the kitchen. Tension rolls off her in waves and finds me across the room. I want to say something magically capable of fixing her bad mood, but I'm no miracle worker.

"Seoul and her kittens were under an empty trailer. Billy found homes for the other kittens, but no one wanted the mom or her two black-and-white boys. So they wouldn't end up at the shelter, I adopted them."

"You're a good person to take on three."

Daisy walks to me, and I notice she's barefoot. I don't know why this realization makes me smile, but I grimace from the motion.

"Tell me you're in pain," she demands.

"I'm in pain, Bourbon Babe."

Daisy's angry expression eases. "Have you taken anything for the pain?"

"Popped a few Tylenol before I came over."

78

"Why *did* you come over?" she asks, crossing her arms.

"I missed you."

Daisy deflates before my eyes. Her arms relax next to her body, and her anger disappears.

"I missed you, too," she mumbles. "Can I sit with you?"

Patting the couch next to me, I wait for her to make her move. Daisy looks at me and where my hand gestures, but she won't budge.

"I'm not fragile," I say.

"You're not indestructible, either."

"No, but I can handle you wrapped around me."

Daisy stares at me, and I have no idea what she's thinking. All these months, I thought about her until I believed I knew her. The truth is she remains a stranger in a million damn ways.

"What are you thinking?" I ask.

"I think you're gorgeous, even with your face kicked in."

"That's very shallow, Daisy," I say, trying not to laugh.

Rolling her eyes, she sits on the couch but keeps her distance. "Your club did this."

"I broke the code."

"So, you could break it in the future and get hurt again?"

"Life is full of pain. I can't avoid it all," I say, reaching out to caress her cheek.

Leaning into my touch, Daisy sighs. "I hate pain."

"Don't cats trip people? You said one of yours caused you to fall against the dresser, right? Well, why have them if you don't want pain? I think you know certain things are worth the suffering."

"What rule did you break, or is that a secret?"

Though the truth will likely freak out Daisy, lying isn't the answer either. "I left a meeting so I could make our date."

"Oh, well, then I understand," she says, giving me a smile and patting my hand. "Are you hungry?"

"Just like that, you're okay?"

"Well, you had a good reason to ditch the meeting. I couldn't handle getting stood up. I'm very emotionally fragile," she says, pulling her knees to her chest and grinning at me. "I'd get beat up for you. I'd also whine so very much about it afterward."

"I'd baby you," I whisper, caressing her bottom lip with my thumb. "I'd kiss every boo-boo and ouchie. Even the hidden ones."

Daisy's smile brightens. "Nice to know they didn't damage your boy-parts."

"No, they did not. Though I made sure Dayton will cry while pissing for a while."

"Can I get you anything?"

"No," I say, noticing how Daisy's nervous again. "Let me see those giant feet you were complaining about."

Even sharing my smile, she doesn't move, so I tug her feet forward until they rest in my lap.

"They're dirty."

"Do I look like I give a shit?"

"A little. I sense you're very concerned about cleanliness."

Smiling at her teasing, I caress her feet. "You'd think big feet would help you balance better, not make you clumsy."

"Yeah, but I never learned to control them. Big feet run in my family. I seemed to get all of my mom's worst qualities, and none of her better ones."

"How do you figure? Sally's a good-looking woman, and you're sexy as fuck."

"Well, sure, I have the sexy thing down," Daisy says, blushing to my surprise. "But she has an easy confidence. She's fearless, too. Mom moved to the US from Brazil when she was seventeen. She taught herself English. She did it all on her own. I'm not independent like that. I'd prefer to have things handed to me."

"Wouldn't we all?" I tease, running my thumb along the arch of her left foot. "We're not so different. My father built the club, while my mother comes from a wealthy, connected family. I've already had so much handed to me. All I need to do is not fuck up what they created."

"That's why you needed to take the beating, right?"

Nodding, I see tears filling Daisy's eyes. "It's not that bad."

"If I was hurt, would you shrug it off?"

"No, I'd fuck someone up."

Daisy struggles not to cry. "You want me to be okay with this, right?"

"I need you to learn to be okay with it, yeah."

"Then, you have to promise me something. No more of that male bravado shit. You can do it with other people. But with me, you tell the truth if you're in pain. I need to know you're square with me."

"In my defense, I didn't know how you'd react, and I wasn't taking a dump on our new relationship."

"Charming."

"Well, relationship talk makes me uncomfortable."

"I don't like it, either. I want everything easy, but I'm not an easy person. I overthink and over-plan everything. I obsess until I freeze up. If you need me to adjust to this new stuff, you need to help me by also adjusting. I'm too lazy to do all the work alone."

"If you can scoot your ass closer and give me a kiss, I'll adjust to anything you want, babe."

Daisy wipes her eyes and maneuvers herself closer. When I pat my lap, she straddles me and stares into my eyes.

"Better?"

"I know I ain't the prettiest thing to look at right now, but I've wanted to kiss you all day. I really prefer never to be denied."

Smiling, Daisy tentatively presses her lips against mine. She's so delicate and careful with her touch, but I'm starving for this woman.

Wrapping my arms around Daisy, I keep her body tightly against mine. My lips take control, and they're anything but tentative. Desperate for her to accept everything I offer, I realize I'm falling for Daisy in a way she better be ready for.

FOURTEEN - DAISY

I taste Camden on my lips long after he leaves my trailer. His scorching touch distracts me from obsessing over his every bruise and swollen flesh. Until the next morning, when I'm bored at work.

Imagining Camden's father, brother, and friends beating on him, I don't understand their reasoning. Why force Camden to behave like a sheep only to turn around in a few years and expect him to be a leader? The entire idea pisses me off, but I'm powerless to step in and protect him.

By the time I get home from work, I'm in a terrible mood. Harmony does her usual routine of trying to make everyone happy so they don't crap on her eternal rainbow-and-unicorn lifestyle.

"Dayton sucks," I tell her as we sit outside her trailer and watch Keanu play with his trucks in the dirt.

"Of course, he does. All of the Rutgers do."

I balk. "Camden doesn't."

"He messed with your car to force you to walk to work, so he could force you to get a ride from him, so he could force you to go out to dinner with him. Oh, and he called you a cock tease plus sabotaged your dates."

Frowning hard at her, I mutter, "I thought you were trying to make me feel better."

"I'm not going to lie."

"You and your no lying crap. Can't you just try?"

"No way. I don't have a good enough memory to keep my lies straight. Best to stick with the truth and make people smile through positive vibes."

"You might need to turn up your vibes since I feel worse now."

"Why are you upset exactly?"

"You saw Camden's face. They beat the heck out of him."

"That's his life. He beat the heck out of them, too. Men like them fight a lot, and they don't take it personally. If you want to be with Camden, you'll need to stop taking it so personally, too."

"He was in pain," I say, my voice breaking.

"I know, and you like to fix things, but there are lots of problems with no fix. Plus, Camden doesn't think of what happened as a problem. He comes from that life. If someone from our family got busted up like that, the rest of us would go nuts. Remember when Betty was dating that guy, and he slapped her?"

After Betty had explained to Sally and Charlie what happened, the three women drove to the guy's house and beat the shit out of him. I doubt my mother and her friends ever considered getting in trouble with the law. Not that the guy planned to call the cops and explain how he got beat down by three middle-aged women.

"True."

"If I might irritate you more, is it possible you're so upset because they harmed Camden's physical appearance, and you're only interested in him for superficial reasons?"

"Why would that question ever irritate me?" I ask, unable to control my sarcasm.

Harmony begins laughing and keeps going until she's snorted twice. "I heard somewhere you were sensitive."

"So, you think I'm so shallow I only want Camden for his looks?"

"Yeah, actually, I did consider that since you two have nothing in common. I mean, I've flirted plenty with Dayton, but I never pretend it's because he and I are soul mates. I just like looking at his handsome face, and he does have a great butt."

"You're not me," I mumble, crossing my arms defensively.

"No, I'm not. I can enjoy a meaningless relationship, and I'm not afraid to have my heart broken. You need things to mean stuff and to feel like you're making the right decisions. You can't just be. It keeps you from enjoying stuff. Like how you got upset at the very idea of dating Camden for his looks. The guy is frigging hot as hell. There's no shame in wanting a sexy man at your disposal. It doesn't have to be anything more than that, but you're pissed at me now."

"I care about Camden."

"I never said you didn't. I only said your interest is superficial, and that's okay. But you think it isn't."

"Well, it isn't."

"Why?"

"I don't know. It's demeaning toward him, I guess."

Harmony bursts into laughter again, and Keanu looks back at her. He's unsure if he ought to laugh, too. His mom is giggling her ass off while I'm frowning like someone died. She waves at him, and he waves back before returning to the world of trucks and blocks.

"Camden doesn't need you to protect his giant ego," Harmony says, wiping her damp eyes. "You know that, too. This isn't about him, but your need to make everything meaningful, especially your first time. That's the real reason you freaked out at Hannah's party. Popping your cherry should involve rose petals and violins playing, not grunting in someone's guest bathroom."

Frowning darker, I consider Harmony's words. She scoots closer to me on the bench.

"Don't be sad."

"You make me sound shallow and stupid."

"No, you're twisting my words into saying you're shallow and stupid. I think it's okay for you to want things to be a certain way. I just want you to know that you feel that way and not to make everything bigger than it is. Why can't you enjoy Camden without feeling he has to be your one true love? It's not like women in our family ever find that guy. Or when they do like Ruby, things don't turn out right. So, enjoy Camden and his good looks without feeling guilty.

After all, he isn't feeling guilty for enjoying your good looks."

"Yeah, butter me up with the compliment thrown in at the end."

"Worked, didn't it?" she asks, nudging me.

"Well, I do enjoy hearing I'm good-looking. I guess I am shallow."

"Everyone wants to feel desirable."

"I guess you could be right about my interest in Camden being completely looks-based."

"Well, not completely. He is pursuing you and buying you flowers and making you feel special. It's not like he's horrible, and you're only enduring him so you can look at his handsome face."

"He is sweet. I didn't expect him to be."

"He's also pushy, which is good since you'd never get anything done if someone didn't kick you in the butt."

"So, I'm lazy now, too?"

"No, you're indecisive."

"That's true."

"I know."

Loosening up, I want to change the subject. "Would you say yes if Dayton asked to have sex?"

"What makes you think he hasn't asked?"

"Because you haven't said yes."

Harmony grins. "I'd probably say yes. Depends on how he asked. I'm perfectly happy with my vibrator. I always go to bed satisfied, while I don't know if Dayton would care as much about my pleasure. He's never had to put someone else first."

"They are spoiled."

"Not their fault. They were raised that way. Plus, they were blessed with good looks and money. Nothing's been hard, so they can't know how spoiled they are."

Hearing kids getting off the bus nearby, I know the sexy talk will need to end soon.

"I like Camden, and I want him to be my first. I have made out sex to be a big deal. I'm not sure anyone will be good enough after all my daydreaming."

"No matter what magical moves Camden possesses, it'll still suck the first time. He's a big guy, and you'll be tense, and that means you're tight down there. It's bound to hurt some, and you'll feel weird and scared. It'll suck, and that's normal. Don't make it mean more than that."

"Any other pointers?"

"Say his name a lot and make sure to look at him. Camden makes you feel good, so remembering you're with him will help with your nerves. If you close your eyes, who knows what might pop in your head."

"Smart."

Harmony pats my hand. "I want you to have fun."

"I have too much of my dad in me. I wish I were more like Mom."

"I like you the way you are. I want you to accept yourself rather than trying to be someone else. There's nothing wrong with Daisy Bourbon Crest."

"That means a lot coming from Harmony Tequila Slater."

"It should. I'm pretty awesome. I mean, look at what I made."

Harmony smiles at Keanu, and I know she wants to play with him. Remaining on the bench, I watch my sister and nephew build LEGO houses. They follow up by crashing into their creations with the trucks. Keanu laughs every time Harmony makes an explosion sound.

This is my sister in a nutshell. Harmony enjoys the small things in life and never sweats the big ones. I sweat everything and enjoy nearly nothing. Life is offering me an exciting adventure with Camden. I'll need to decide whether to embrace the fun or overthink it to death.

FIFTEEN - DAISY

Camden looks a million times better when he arrives at my trailer for dinner. The man must have superhero Viking healing powers. I kiss him hello, hating to let him go. Still rattled from yesterday, I'm terrified to lose him.

"Damn, someone wants a piece of the Cam Man," he says when I keep him wrapped in my arms. "Wait until you see what I brought."

Ignoring his self-assigned nickname, I examine the takeout bags he's carrying. "I'm intrigued."

"Had to go to White Horse to find a Vietnamese restaurant, and I had no damn idea what to order. I ended up getting a little of everything. While it's not cave diving, at least you can enjoy the cuisine like a world traveler."

Camden's good looks aren't why my heart beats violently in my chest. He went through the trouble of bringing me this food based on some throwaway comment I made days ago. Any other guy would buy pizza to please a carb-starved chick. Not Camden.

This sexy man feels all wrong standing in my trailer. As usual, he's perfection, even wearing a simple blue shirt, black jeans, and a bruised face. Camden glances up to notice how close his head is to the trailer's ceiling.

After setting the food bags on my kitchen counter, he smiles back at me. "I think I'll kick off my boots and give myself a little more headroom."

"Have at it," I mumble, overwhelmed by his gesture.

Camden removes his boots and sets them at the front door. "Don't worry, babe. My feet don't stink."

"Of course, they don't."

When his gaze focuses on me, I struggle to smile or say something—anything—but end up only staring like a lovestruck doofus. Camden cups my face in his massive hands, and I open my mouth to speak. Nothing leaves my lips, so he covers them with his.

His tongue touches mine, sending shockwaves through my every nerve. I grab onto him, nearly jumping on his body like a startled cat into a tree. Camden's lips curve into a smile, and he no doubt enjoys knowing I'm mush for him. Any chance at playing our relationship cool has long since passed. So, I wrap him tighter in my arms and nearly hump his left leg.

"You missed me," he says when our lips part.

"No," I mumble, unable to concentrate on anything beyond the warmth between my legs. "What?"

"Thinking is overrated," he teases, patting my ass.

"You went to White Horse to get me dinner."

"It was a twenty-minute drive with traffic. No biggie."

Despite his words, Camden wants me to admire his effort.

"This means a lot. I'd never have the courage to try it alone or even take my sisters. If they didn't like it, I'd feel guilty."

"Well, if I don't like it, I don't want you feeling bad. It's one meal, and I'll probably eat two more before I crash."

"Two?"

"I took a few painkillers last night before bed because I'm a fucking pussy. Ended up sleeping all day and only got up a few hours ago. This is my lunch."

"How are you feeling?"

Camden wants to act tough but remembers what I said the night before about being straight with me.

"My knee hurts like a fucker, but I'm good, otherwise."

"How are Dayton's balls?"

Camden smirks. "He was limping when I saw him in the condo hallway. I bet he was up half the night crying like a bitch."

"You should be very proud," I say while retrieving plates from the cabinet.

Camden's stomach growls so loudly that I add extra servings to his plate. When he takes his food, our fingers touch and share a shock of electricity.

"My bed is in the next room," I blurt out.

"Thanks for the info, but we're not doing anything in that bed tonight," Camden says, walking to the table. He digs his fork into the pile of noodles. "You don't trust me yet. Once you do, I'll take you to bed, and you'll forget other men exist."

"I can safely say I'm already there."

"Not just yet. Sit down and eat. I expect you to try everything."

I join him at the kitchen table and mumble, "Yes, sir."

"I like that," he says, running his fingers through my hair. "Not the 'sir' shit, but you indulging."

"So, you don't want me to obey you?"

"Most definitely, but I want you to want to do what I want you to do but not because I told you to do it." We share a smile at his insane comment before he says, "Eat up."

Obeying him because I want to obey him, I dig into the food. We try everything he ordered. Some we like. A few we spit out.

While gobbling up the rice with Hainan chicken, I realize I'm more nervous tonight than I've been the entire time I've spent with Camden. I'm thinking about sex. Also, whether I'm only interested in him for superficial reasons. Plus, how can I find out if he's only interested in me to scratch the itch I gave him at Hannah's party?

"Thank you," I say, my voice breaking at the thought of one day not being part of his life.

Camden's brown eyes widen. "Please don't cry. I have no shield against a woman's tears."

"I won't. I only want you to know I appreciate you going through all this trouble. It took thought and effort."

Twisting his lips, Camden pretends to be offended. "Am I so dumb and lazy that a trip to the next town to pick up food is something amazing?"

"Yes," I say, laughing at his expression.

Camden smiles at my amusement. "I'm no hero for bringing dinner, but if you want to reward me with couch kisses later, I'm totally fine with that."

Despite his words, I'm overwhelmed by his thoughtfulness. The only people who've ever treated me so well were my mom, sisters, and Lush Gardens family. Even my dad forgets my birthday lately. I know I've put Camden on a pedestal, but his behavior today is addictively perfect.

"I'm glad you're happy," he says after a few minutes. "You were dying to freak out last night, but you kept your cool. I decided to do something special to reward you, and going down on you will have to wait."

"Hold up, why isn't that option available tonight?"

Camden smirks, and his gaze focuses hard on my mouth. I suspect he's thinking about me going down on him.

"You're making me want to puke," I mutter.

"And that's why we have to wait to go to your bedroom."

"Well done."

Camden only smiles and finishes his meal. As soon as I take my last bite, his hand reaches for mine. We walk to the couch where I sit, and he squats in front of me.

"Based on your expression, you're thinking too much. Let's turn off your brain so you can enjoy the night. I'll keep the key to your gray matter in my pocket and give it back before I leave."

Caressing his forearms, I smile. "What if I need to save your life but can't come up with a plan because I don't have the key to my brain?"

"I'll be a dead man, and you'll be a mellow chick."

"If you're okay with that outcome, I am, too."

"Look at how you're already mellowing out."

I watch him put the imaginary key in his jean pocket. When his gaze finds mine, I shiver at the heat in his eyes.

"You look tired," he says, pressing me back on the couch. "You should rest."

91

I open my mouth to disagree, but he pats his pocket to remind me how my brain shouldn't be working. When I still consider speaking, he plants a hot kiss on my lips. By the time our mouths part, I'm beyond relaxed.

Camden rests between my open thighs. "What color is your bra?" he murmurs, sliding up my shirt. "My guess is white."

Breathing faster, I shiver when his fingers tease the loose fabric of my white bra.

"Don't you dare suck in your stomach," he warns and kisses my belly button. "You think too much about your body when you should focus on mine."

My hands rest limply at my sides, but his words force them to find his wide shoulders.

"The fact is, you and I will soon spend many long hours, maybe even days, undressed around each other," he says in a possessive voice. "There'll be no sucking in guts or working angles," he adds before gently biting at my stomach.

My hips react instantly, wiggling under him. Camden arrogantly smiles at my reaction.

"This is my stomach," he says, holding my gaze. "It belongs to me. Do you understand?"

Maybe I nod, but my mind remains hazy with lust. With Camden's flawless face only inches from mine, I watch him as if in a dream.

"This nipple belongs to me, too," he murmurs, and his index finger slides over the hard flesh hiding under my lacy bra. "This one is also mine. No one can touch them except you and me. Do you understand?"

I know I nod this time because my agreement leads to his lips finding mine. Gripping his shoulders, I moan while his fingers tease my nipples.

"I like when you touch me there."

Camden frowns. "Where? You'll have to be more specific."

Smirking, I shrug. "I don't know the name of the part."

"Can you touch the spot you like, so I'll know?"

My fingers tap my nipple. "There."

Camden's thumb grazes my hard flesh. "I want to take this bra off you tonight."

"Why don't you?"

"You're not ready."

"Whatever you say, sir."

Camden smiles wider at me. "Last time, I got greedy. You nearly broke my dick, and we didn't speak for months. I refuse to have a repeat."

"Because you care," I say, holding his gaze. "Because this isn't a game."

"Yes, because I care," he says, staring hard into my eyes as if daring me not to believe. "No, this isn't a game."

"Well, all right then."

Sensing he's won, Camden kisses me and doesn't let up for an hour. His lips suck at mine. Once they reach my neck, I realize I'm ticklish as hell. Camden loves the way I squirm and sucks harder.

"Shit," he says, backing off.

"Did you hurt your mouth giving me a hickey?" I ask, staring dazed at him.

"I'm about to jizz in my pants."

"That's romantic," I say, caressing his chest. "Do you want to go to my bedroom now?"

"Nope." Camden shrinks away. "I need a minute or two to get myself under control."

"But I want you to lose control."

"Not really. What girl wants a guy to come five seconds into their first fuck?"

Frowning now, I glance back at my bed and imagine him naked.

Camden runs his hands through his hair and sighs. "This weekend is the Brotherhood's chili cook-off. I want you to meet the guys and see the club isn't a scary thing."

"I want to have sex."

A scowling Camden glances at my door as if ready to escape. "I get how you're a horny chick. However, there's a time and place to rip off our clothes, and now isn't it."

"I'm serious."

"I am, too."

"It's important to me to get it done."

Camden looks genuinely irritated now. "I'm trying to build something here beyond carnal desires. Can't you stop thinking with your crotch long enough to give my idea a try?"

"Don't play coy. You're the one about to jizz in his pants, so I know you want this too. If you won't do it tonight, let me come to your place tomorrow. We'll pop my cherry and see what happens."

"What do you mean by what happens?"

Crossing my arms, I catch Camden's gaze lock on my boobs pressed together.

"Look, I know my first time will likely suck. I'll be nervous, and you're large. So, I don't expect to be blown away. The next few times will be awkward as I get the hang of your giant manhood. After that, I'll enjoy the sex. I want to know what happens after we scratch our itches."

"So, you think you'll lose interest once I put out?"

"Maybe. We don't have anything in common."

Camden stands up and adjusts his jeans. "I don't have shit in common with any woman. I'm a fucking guy, Daisy. But I'm not looking to fuck another me."

"Aren't you curious about what happens after the sex?"

"I just assumed you hold me while I cried."

Fighting laughter, I stand up and fix my shirt. "I promise I'll comfort you if you need to let out your emotions."

"You're a sweet chick."

"So, can we do it tomorrow?"

"I don't know. I'm not accustomed to jumping into a stranger's bed. Like you said, we don't really know each other."

"Oh, for fuck's sake, stop teasing me."

Camden grins at my anger. "Haven't you ever wanted something so much it was worth doing everything right?"

"I don't care about that. I've got sex on the brain. Until I get laid, I can't focus on much else."

"You are a horny little babe, aren't you?" he says, taking a lock of my hair and twirling it around his finger.

"So, can we do it tomorrow?"

"I guess. I mean, I'll try to get in the mood, but a man needs to be romanced."

"I'll bring flowers, you big baby."

"Real pretty ones?" he asks, batting his sexy eyes.

"Why are you making this so difficult?"

"Because you're planning shit that shouldn't be planned."

"Grownups plan things, Camden. We crave control over our lives."

"You do? I don't."

"Because things happen easily for you. If you had to work for everything, you'd plan shit, too."

"You sure think my life is all peaches and roses."

"Peaches?"

"You've got me thinking of sex now."

"So, can I come to your place tomorrow and enjoy your hunkiness?"

"Sure, but only if you're feeling it. I don't want you acting as if fucking is an assignment. I never liked homework, and I won't make our relationship a job."

"Relationships involve work. Didn't you say something about how your dad never worked on his relationship with your mom?"

Camden steps closer and teases my left nipple. "Yeah, but that was when things got tough. Things right now aren't that way between us, so why make it feel like work?"

"Whatever. Just put out tomorrow, and we'll see what happens."

"Yes, ma'am."

Glancing down at how he gently tugs at my nipple, I say, "You should leave. I need to take a shower and masturbate. Probably not in that order."

"You're cruel when denied," Camden grumbles, stepping back and walking to where his boots rest. "I should probably get home and jerk it a few times."

"I'd like to watch you jerk it some time."

Camden narrows his eyes. "You're teetering into evil territory, young lady."

I smile and adjust my bra. "I offered, but you said no. A girl can get blue balls, too."

"No, they really can't. Besides, we both know you'll thank me one day for not popping your cherry tonight."

"That's probably true, but I'm too horny to currently care."

Camden kisses my forehead. "Horny is so fucking beautiful on you."

"Tomorrow, you won't stop, right?" I ask, wrapping my arms around him possessively.

"Not as long as you don't."

"Fair enough. Thanks for the Vietnamese food and making my nipples dance in joy."

Camden groans quietly. "My dick is ready to tear through these jeans."

"Well, you better go then. Can I have the key to my brain back?"

"Nope. You don't need it. Until I see you, just sit around, looking beautiful."

Rolling my eyes, I start to follow him outside, but Camden stops me. He cups my face and gives me one more lingering kiss before stepping back.

"My self-control is slipping."

"See you tomorrow then," I say, caressing his swollen lip.

Camden awkwardly walks away from my trailer, and I suspect his erection will make the ride home a painful one.

While my pants aren't too snug, my panties are most definitely drenched.

SIXTEEN - DAISY

My body buzzes with excitement even before I step into Camden's condo. I've spent the last day imagining us naked. Everything is planned in my head. After arriving home from work, I spent an hour grooming. While I view waxing my lady lush in the realm of self-mutilation, I did embrace the less violent Nair option. I don't know how great my once jungle-like nether regions look, but at least Camden won't need a machete to find his way to the sweet spot.

"What do you think?" Camden asks once he shuts the door to his place.

I look around the condo with its high ceilings, dark floors, cabinets and countertops, and black furniture. There's no denying a guy lives here, but I do notice a lack of personal touches.

"It smells like you."

"It ought to. I scent it every day, just like your cats."

Staring up at him, I nod. "I bet you do," I say, breathless from terror. "Let's do this."

Camden sidesteps my horny hands. "Chill the jets, babe. Let's have a drink and talk first."

"Talk about what?" I mutter, hiding none of my annoyance.

"How was your day?"

"Fine. Yours?"

"Frustrating, but it improved when I picked you up."

Smiling, I tug off my shirt with my trembling hands. "That's sweet. Thanks for the chat. Let's do this thing."

Camden opens his mouth to tell me to calm down or cool off or something again about jets. I don't know what he intends to say, but the sight of my bra clicks his brain into neutral.

"That's right," I say, shaking my hips. "Come to me, beast man, and take what I offer."

"You're a natural with dirty talk," he mumbles, watching me while I kick off my sandals.

"Oh, yeah, babble over here, buddy."

Camden shakes his head, trying to pry his gaze from the sight of my bra. "I can make you a screwdriver if you'd like."

"I want your screw to drive me into happiness."

Camden fights laughter. "I'll make you a drink."

I stomp my foot like a pissed toddler. "Why are you playing shy, man-slut? Give me what I want."

"Or what?" he asks from his shiny clean kitchen.

"I'll whine more. You don't even want to know how much I can whine."

"Show me," he murmurs in a deep, sexy voice that pisses me off.

"I get it. I mean, you've fucked millions of women, so tonight is no big deal for you. This is my first time, and I want it fucking now. But your dick is satisfied from the concert hall full of women you've screwed," I grumble and then add, "You're selfish."

"Horniness sure makes you grouchy."

Crossing my arms, I stare down at my boobs and wonder if the crease is sweaty from the ride over. Should I shower again? I spent a half hour under the water, scrubbing myself clean, but I might need a quick refresh.

Camden walks to me and places a glass in my hand. I stare into his dark eyes and wish he would fuck me already so I can stop wondering.

"You're thinking too much. I need to steal the key to your brain again. No more worrying. Just relax."

"I'd relax more if I was properly serviced by an experienced lover."

His fingers caress my cheek, sending hot signals to the rest of my body. I glance down at where my nipples harden as if on command.

"See how good you are?" I whisper, staring at Camden. "You make me feel sexy. That's all I want. To feel pretty

99

and special," I explain as my fingers caress his jaw like he does mine. "Now, get naked."

Camden flashes a brilliant smile but steps back like a cold-hearted vagina tease. I take a big gulp of the screwdriver while he picks up my shirt and presses it against his lips. Inhaling, he still smiles at me.

"I love your scent."

"I love yours, too," I mutter, annoyed by how he's letting my enthusiasm crash and burn.

"If you were still dressed, I'd show you the balcony with the view of Hickory Creek."

Gulping down more of the drink, I shrug. "Maybe that would interest other chicks, but I don't care about the view. Other women might be impressed by your money, but I'm only interested in your good looks. And the way you touch me," I say and sigh. "And the way you say my name. I'm interested in Camden stuff, not the family money stuff."

As Camden studies me, I see a dent in his calm exterior. "You really don't care about the money?"

"Why would I? I plan to spend my life living at the trailer park. Don't need money for that."

Though Camden nearly rolls his eyes at my big life plans, he valiantly restrains the urge. "I want you, Daisy, and not because I have an itch to scratch."

"Yeah, I've noticed," I say and then chug the rest of the drink. "Now, will you get naked?"

"I want to see you naked first," he says, taking the empty glass before easing into his giant chair. "You're partway there. Shimmy out of those shorts."

"Are you trying to kill my good mood?" I ask, crossing my arms.

Camden doesn't answer. His gaze roams up and down my body, undressing me mentally. I wonder what he sees and if I can live up to his expectations.

"Stop thinking," he finally says.

"You try to stop thinking and see how easy it is."

"I don't think. I just do."

"Profound," I sigh, tightening my arms across my chest. "Can't you at least take off your shirt before I strip down?"

Camden yanks off his shirt in one smooth movement. I bask into the brilliance of this man's tanned chest and ache to run my fingers through the splash of dark hair.

"Don't fade out on me," he teases, leaning back as if watching a football game. "Let's make this easy for you, babe. Take off your shorts."

I don't hesitate. My gaze remains focused on him while I pop the button on my denim shorts. They fall to the ground, and I kick them away.

"Is it your turn now?" I ask, imagining his powerful thighs.

"Nope. I want you to get over your nerves by stripping down."

My eyes go wide at the thought of being so exposed. "That sounds nerve-wracking. How in the hell is it supposed to help me?"

"Lose the bra and you'll see."

"A whole lot of bossy crap if you ask me," I mutter under my breath.

"What was that?"

Rolling my eyes, I reach back and unsnap my bra. I open my mouth to apologize for not having bigger boobs or being hotter or whatever. The words come out in French, which makes Camden smile since he has no idea what I'm saying.

Despite my cheeks flushed with embarrassment, I focus on getting through the stripping routine. That way, I'll gain access to his muscular chest.

I toss the bra next to my shorts. "I have breasts," I announce in English, though the words sound more empowering in my head.

"That you do," he says in a voice that screams he's a fan of the view.

Less self-conscious, I grab the sides of my black panties and shimmy them down my legs. Once I'm naked, I put my arms in the air.

"I am officially naked in Camden Rutgers's house."

"Fucking-A, you are," he says, standing up.

For a split second, I think he'll make a run for it. Or pull a prank to punish me for running out on him at the party. My panic passes once logic reminds me how he wouldn't waste time on such a long con.

Camden walks directly to me, cups my face, and plants a hot kiss on my lips. Everything falls away around us. I turn into a puddle of heat, wanting more from him. No longer thinking, I enjoy Camden's command of my body.

He effortlessly lifts me, and my legs wrap around his waist. I shudder at how good he tastes. No other man kisses like Camden. No other man does *anything* like Camden. I don't care how long this ride lasts. I plan to enjoy the scenery.

Camden carries me somewhere, but I'm blinded to everything beyond our bodies. The feel of my nipples against his coarse chest hair sends a wave of heat through me, and my hips roll reflexively against his.

Moaning into my mouth, Camden tightens his hold on me. His lips demand my full attention, and I submit to Camden as he rests me on his massive bed.

Rather than feeling exposed, I've let down my guard for Camden. He deserves everything he desires, and I will give him anything he asks. I only want more time in the presence of my sexy Viking.

Camden holds my gaze while yanking off his thick black belt, faded blue jeans, and plain white boxers. I can't help glancing down to where he exposes himself the way I did minutes earlier.

"Red alert," I mumble, crawling away from him and against the headboard. "Abort mission. Nope, not happening."

Camden only smiles at my panic. "Your pussy will be ready by the time my cock takes what you've saved for me."

I gape at his massive penis and wonder if I'll walk normally again once he's done with me. *Can my dream and his dick co-exist?*

After taking a deep breath, I slowly exhale. "I like when you say pussy."

Camden never falters. He doesn't react to my panic. He only stands before me buck naked with too many muscles and too giant of a cock. I realize he's telling the truth about never thinking. For him, life is something he consumes, dominates, and even wrecks when necessary.

"What do I do?" I ask, crawling back to the end of the bed.

"Nothing," he says tenderly as his fingers slide hair off my shoulders. "Don't think or try to be sexy. Just relax and let me do everything. I promise you'll be happy in the end."

Reaching up for him, I relax into his embrace. His lips cover mine, and I'm less aware of the massive cock poking at me. Sure, I know it's there, and I can still feel it mocking me. I suspect I'll either worship or fear his cock by the end of the day. Hell, I'll likely do both.

SEVENTEEN - CAMDEN

Daisy's frightened eyes watch my every move. I want to hold her gaze. Yes, I should reassure my girl, but her naked flesh calls out to me. *How can I deny its desire for my attention?*

My fingers skim the soft curves of her hips, and a blissful Daisy mercifully closes her eyes. Unlocking my gaze from hers, I focus on the sweet mounds of flesh I've wanted to taste for too long.

Daisy's tits lift and fall with her every breath. My tongue coats her perky pink nipple with my saliva. Daisy's breathing immediately increases. I glance up to find her eyes still closed. She's already overwhelmed by the sensations I've awakened in her body.

Pressing her soft tits together, I taste one nipple and then the other. Daisy wiggles and moans in French, but her eyes remain shut. She softly says my name when I nibble at her left nipple. She simply sighs when I suck at the right one.

My lips tease and torment her nipples until Daisy whimpers and reaches for her pussy. I follow her fingers and find damp flesh waiting for me.

Her folds are slick, and the sweet scent makes my mouth water. I want to dive in and devour her. Gripping the sheets, I force my tongue only to lick at where her clit begs for me to taste. Inhaling harshly, I can barely keep my dick from taking control. Her flavor sends me into a fucking trance. I only want more.

Diving deeper, my tongue eagerly savors Daisy's pussy. I hear her crying out, and she tries to close her legs. My hands keep her thighs open wide. Knowing she'll only settle down once she comes, I suck at her folds, licking deep into her virginal entrance. Fighting the pleasure, Daisy still begs, but she doesn't know what she wants or needs. My Bourbon Babe is heady with desire and can't control her body's reaction.

Licking wildly at her clit, I relish the sounds of Daisy losing control. Her words make no sense. I glance up to see her flushed face in a state of panicked bliss. She's so close, and I want to watch her come apart.

My gaze focuses on her face as I suck her engorged clit. Daisy's mouth opens, wanting to cry out. The moan catches in her chest, and a shudder rolls through her luscious body. I watch her struggle against the intensity. Sucking deeply, I know she's still coming from the rush of juices against my face. Daisy only cries out as the orgasm fades.

"Camden," she finally says as if returning from the heaven my mouth sent her to. "It's too much."

"No, you need this," I say, pressing a finger into her tight hole.

Daisy groans at my probing. Her gaze finds me, and she shakes her head.

"I can't do this. It's too much."

I crawl over her until our lips are an inch apart. "Take what your body craves."

Kissing her, I slide my cock along her wet slit. I don't know if she's ready for me, but I'm fucking certain I can't wait any longer. A few more minutes of her flavor on my tongue, and I'll come on her stomach.

"I need to fuck you," I whisper and lick Daisy's juices from her lips. "I need to open you up and take what you've saved for me."

"Yes," she says, even looking terrified. "I'm scared, but yes."

Kneeling between her legs, I caress her clit with the head of my cock. The tender nub glistens with my pre-cum, and her pussy clenches from the pleasure. Positioning the head against her entrance, I fill her only an inch before pausing to enjoy her clenching muscles.

Daisy licks her lips, nearly enticing my balls to let go of their load. I close my eyes to regain control. I want to come deep inside her. Not like this, not until she takes everything I can offer.

Focused again, I open my eyes and find a wide-eyed Daisy watching me.

"You need to be fucked," I murmur in a rough voice.

Even nodding, Daisy remains afraid. I feel her pussy clamping around my cock, wanting to expel me from her body. My dick refuses rejection. With a small thrust, I gain another inch.

"My Bourbon Babe needs to be fucked," I growl, reaching forward to tug at her still wet nipples.

"Yes," she says, and her pussy relaxes enough for me to gain another two inches. "Please," she whimpers.

"Please fuck you? Is that what you want?"

Daisy doesn't know what she wants. Hot and soaking wet, her pussy both welcomes and rejects me.

"Close your eyes," I order when her fearful gaze cut through my confidence.

Obeying, Daisy closes her eyes and swallows hard. I thrust slowly into her pussy, stretching her tight flesh while tugging at her erect nipples.

Her body gives me more until I'm as deep inside as my size can fit. Clenching rhythmically around my cock, her pussy aches to be fucked, and I can't hold back any longer.

Propping myself over her, I thrust deep and steady. My hips find a rhythm, wanting to prolong the exquisite pressure of her vise-like pussy.

"It's okay, Camden," Daisy says, startling me.

Her gaze holds mine, and I understand she wants me to let go.

My hips never hesitate, immediately thrusting harder and faster. I need to come inside her and claim what she offers me. No man can ever know this feeling with Daisy.

Grunting at the increased pressure, Daisy watches me in curious horror. I fuck her hard. I'm past going slow. My patience and tender touch are gone. I'm a man unhinged with only fucking on his mind.

I've wanted Daisy for too long. Her body already belongs to me, yet now I make it submit. Fucking fast and hard, I expect to come, but my dick begs for more time. I need to enjoy her sucking pussy around my cock. I can't stop. Not yet. Fuck her harder, faster, more and more until I can't think.

My orgasm takes me by surprise. I'm at the peak of pain and pleasure when my balls unleashed their load into her waiting body. Daisy's nails dig into my forearms as I bear down on her, filling her pussy with my cum.

I yell out her name, unable to form any other word. She's all I see, feel, and know as the orgasm tears through me and somehow infects her. Daisy cries out, sounding terrified by the way her body betrays her. We're both slaves to our carnal desires at this moment. Coming and coming, we're like one animal bound together.

I rest over her, still thrusting gently long after my orgasm passes. Daisy watches me horrified. When I think to pull from her, though, she grips my ass to keep me in place. Her pussy sucks approvingly at my cock. The disconnect between her body and brain is apparent from her expression.

"I can't stop," I whisper, reaching between us to squeeze her nipples. "I need more."

"Take more," she moans. "What are you waiting for?"

Grinning, I cover Daisy's mouth with mine and devour her moans as I thrust harder into her. Our bodies don't care about the future or past. They're indifferent to heartfelt promises. They only crave more pleasure until they see nothing else.

EIGHTEEN - DAISY

So, this is what all the fuss is about. Sex never interested me as much as it did every other girl at school. They were dying to lose their virginity and "become a woman." Somehow, I crawled my way into adulthood with my cherry intact. Deep inside, I assumed sex was likely overrated, and no one was brave enough to admit it.

Okay, so I was wrong.

Camden knows his way around a woman's body, but he tells me after our second round how everyone is different. I feel special when he says that. He must sense my annoyance. His lips curl into a smile before finding my nipple and sucking hard enough to make me stupid.

My nipples were never the least bit sensitive until they met Camden's scorching mouth. Even his perfect white teeth make them sing with pleasure. I watch him nibble, lick, and suck at a part of my body I've shown so little attention to during my entire twenty-four years on earth. I feel guilty now as if I've neglected them. How could I know my nipples wanted love when they gave me the cold shoulder until Camden?

I'm self-conscious about my body for the first ten minutes in bed. Once I manage to fit his massive meat inside me, I become fearless.

Resting on my back, I smile at him. "I want a shirt saying, 'I survived Camden Rutgers's giant dong.' I think people would respect me more if they saw that. Of course, plenty of women own that shirt."

Camden stops playing with my canoe-sized feet and exhales hard. "I didn't want to say anything. I was nervous, I guess. I think you deserve the truth now."

I frown at him, worried until I remember Camden is a sexy bastard who enjoys playing mind games.

"I'll try to be understanding," I murmur, nudging him with my foot.

"I'm a virgin. Or at least, I was until today. Don't judge me."

Laughing behind my hand, I whisper, "I had a feeling."

"All of those rumors about me were my way of protecting my ego," he says, earnestly selling his bullshit.

"Of course. Poor Camden. I'll keep your secret."

Grinning, he studies my foot. "Do you ever get pedicures?"

"No. Why?"

"You should pamper yourself."

"Is that your way of saying my feet are disgusting?"

"No. I see my mom pamper herself, and I want you to do the same. You deserve everything."

"Oh, well, that's sweet, but I don't like having my feet touched." When Camden studies my foot, I grin. "I didn't say stop."

"Whatever you want, cherry popper."

Laughing, I close my eyes as he licks at the bottom of my foot. "Why would you ever want to do that?"

"To see if it makes you hot. How will a virgin like me learn anything if I don't try?"

"Very true. Should I lick your feet now so I can learn?"

"If you're looking to lick something, I have another spot in mind."

"I have a sensitive gag reflex," I warn and sit up. "So be careful."

"First, you threaten to pee on me. Now, you claim you might barf on me. You make sexy look effortless."

Giggling wildly at how I once threatened to pee on him, I never seem to control my brain when Camden's around. He makes me blurt out stupid stuff left and right.

"Sorry for the visual, but the warning is real."

Camden strokes my hair, wrapping it gently in his hand. "You lead. I'll sit back and enjoy."

"What if I mess up?" I ask, wrapping my hands around his resting cock. "I'm afraid I might bite it."

"I'm afraid of that, too, but we'll figure it out."

Looking up at him, I smile and run my tongue across my teeth. "You're a very patient teacher. I imagine learning many things from you, even if you were so very recently a virgin."

Camden looks ready to spout another line of sexy bullshit. Just until I cautiously lick the head of his dick. Now, he's stunned into silence, relieving me of my cheer section.

I'm terrified of injuring him. All my life, I've heard men are sensitive in the crotch-region. I don't know anything otherwise about their franks and beans. The closest I got to touching one before Camden was while changing Keanu's diapers. I'm ill-equipped for performing a blowjob, and I consider backing out.

Camden's dick hardens in my hands, giving me confidence. It likes me, and I could learn to like it, too. We could be the best of friends if I just get over my fear. I tentatively lick the head and then the base. I even kiss his balls, but I have no rhythm.

"I'm sorry," I say, blushing beet red.

"You're fascinating to watch."

"I'm taking that as a compliment."

"I've never enjoyed a blowjob more than this one."

"I thought you were a virgin."

Camden smirks. "Oh, yeah, well, I think even if I wasn't, this is still the best."

"You just don't want me to stop."

"Stop or don't. Either way, you and I aren't done playing undressed, Miss Bourbon."

"Well, all right then."

I return to licking his now thick, angry-looking cock. At the head is a drip of cum, and I lick it off. When the taste doesn't kill me, I lick the drop taking the first one's place. I'm too inexperienced, and his dick is too big for me to work the entire thing into submission. Instead, I focus only on the manageable mushroom-shaped head.

Every drop of cum is a reward. I want to make him feel as good as he did me. His cock throbs in my hand as I suck steadily at the head. When I feel overwhelmed, I graze the slit with the tip of my tongue. Camden moans, encouraging me. I suck again and close my eyes.

The world falls away, and I'm alone in the blissful abyss with my addictive Viking. He's weak from my touch, moaning louder as I take him closer to the edge.

I need everything he can give me. Camden is my one shot at amazing in my otherwise average life. He deserves to lose his mind, even if only for a moment. I want to be the woman to make him forget all the others. Maybe a blowjob isn't enough for them to disappear, but I don't care about reality right now. My only goal in life is to have him come hard with my name on his lips.

NINETEEN - CAMDEN

Daisy is the picture of delicate beauty as I move inside her body. Her face reveals her every emotion. Waves of pleasure compel her eyes to close and her lips to part so perfectly. I'm addicted to how her body responds to my touch.

I've never been a man interested in cherry popping. There's too much pressure for me to wrangle a woman's feelings. Daisy's virginity is a double-edged sword. While I don't want another man to know her body, I'm wary of pushing her too far.

Once her body is hot and wet, Daisy meets my hunger with her increasingly confident one. Our bodies find a rhythm, learning to work together to find pleasure.

When she shows off her oral skills, I mentally laugh at my stupidity. Daisy is a grown woman and perfectly capable of telling me what she wants. More than once, she warns of her gag reflex even while she sucks me off like an enthusiastic pro.

"You're mine," I tell her when she straddles me. "I waited a long time for you, and I don't plan to give you up."

"Okay."

"This isn't sex talk. I'm serious about keeping you."

"You do that," she says, rubbing her wet pussy against my soft cock.

Watching her experiment with our bodies, I realize the best part of her inexperience. Everything she does is new. Her second time will be her first, second time, and I'll be right here to witness her reactions. The first time she sucked off a guy, I was the one to enjoy her proud expression. Daisy isn't jaded by sex. Her new experiences wash away my past sexual deeds. I start over with Daisy and never see anyone else.

The next day, I relish in my well-fucked bliss until I run into Dayton. My mood immediately sours when he mentions the pizza place and how Howler's already named the future strip club.

"Ain't happening."

"Mom can't veto club business," Dayton says, sitting next to me at the restaurant counter. "She knows that, so she whined to us."

"I'm telling her that you said she whines."

Dayton grins. "She knows I talk shit about everyone. I got that rumor-spreading habit from the Hallstead side of the family. If she doesn't like it, she ought to look in the mirror."

"I don't want another strip club in Hickory Creek. We already have too many fucking bail bonds and gold for cash places. A new no-credit loan place opened across the street from Daisy's work. As if we don't have enough low-class businesses in Hickory Creek, Howler wants to add a strip club."

Shrugging, Dayton steals one of my fries. "He wants to make money that's going to Common Bend and the Reapers Motorcycle Club."

"We need to decide if Hickory Creek will be a low-rent Common Bend shithole with meth heads and whores on every corner. Or do we want to aim higher like in White Horse where they court real family businesses and bring in a better class of people?"

"You're a low-class fuck. Does that mean you plan to move out so a fancy fuck can take your place in Hickory Creek?"

"You know I'm right."

"I know a lot of things, but I ain't sharing jack-shit with you, brother."

"What's up your ass?" I ask when I realize he's serious.

Dayton turns and glares hard at me. I'd be intimidated if I hadn't seen him shit his pants when we were kids.

"Dad hasn't retired, yet you're already walking around as if you're club president. You don't discuss with Dad or Howler what Mom wants. You just tell them what she wants, like she's running the club."

"Is this Dad talking?" I ask, flicking a ketchup-covered fry at my pissed brother. "This sounds like him bitching about the Hallstead family influencing his business. We've been hearing him gripe since we were kids."

"He isn't wrong."

Turning on the stool to face Dayton, I say, "The Brotherhood is protected by the sheriff. Our aunt, I might remind you, says so. She covers our asses. That's the Hallstead power. Our other aunt is the mayor, and she watches for state pressure to mess with our businesses. Hallstead blood protects the club. We're Hallsteads. Howler is, too. Dad doesn't like them pissing in our playground, but he's the one who invited them to drop their pants long ago. Now, he's whining about their leaky bladders."

"What's with all your piss talk?"

I think about how Daisy needs to pee after every ride on Shasta. The girl's bladder is the size of a peanut, and any jiggling makes her do the potty dance.

No way will I share this info with Dayton. If I'd kept my mouth shut months ago, Daisy's confidence would be stronger, and I'd have claimed her earlier.

"Do you not want me to be president?" I ask Dayton, ignoring his question.

"Why does everyone assume it should be you?"

"Who else would it be?"

"Uh, me, ass-fuck."

I frown at him, wondering if I missed a conversation at some point where he expressed his desire to lead.

"Since when do you give a shit about running the club?"

"Since always."

"You lie like a fucking twat."

"Fine. I've gotten to thinking about it recently."

"Why?"

"Why not?"

Shrugging, I never once imagined Dayton taking the Brotherhood president role. In the right mood, the guy can get mean as fuck, but he never once showed interest in calling the shots.

"Well then, when the time comes, throw in your hat for the job and see what happens."

"I will."

"Good for you, monkey-shit."

Dayton smirks. "You've got toilets on the brain."

"Probably. I had breakfast at IHOP with Daisy, and the place was crawling with stink machines. I can still smell them. Might need to shower to wash it off."

"Family life is disgusting."

"Good thing Mom and Dad didn't think that, idiot."

"You're the idiot."

"How do you figure?"

Dayton stands up and shrugs. "I don't know. I just always thought you were stupid. Never could put my finger on why."

"Don't you want to stick around and eat?"

"With you? No. I'm avoiding people who piss me off."

"Then, you're doing a shitty job since you walked over to me."

"Yeah, yeah. See you tonight at the chili cook-off."

"I'm bringing Daisy, so be on your best behavior."

My brother rolls his eyes, slaps a few bucks on the counter for his coffee, and walks out of the diner. I watch him go and wonder if I should be concerned about him having my back. While Dayton isn't the type of man to kill his brother, I can imagine a few scenarios where he'd at least wound me.

TWENTY - CAMDEN

Over the years, Daisy's visited Salty Peanuts on several occasions. This is her first time as my woman. She gnaws wildly on her gum until I finally have her spit it out. When she begins chewing on her bottom lip, I kiss Daisy.

My affection leaves Daisy rosy-cheeked as we walk into the bar. Her mind is on my lips rather than the club or chili. I do notice her interest piques once the aroma of slow-cooked beans finds us.

"My girl loves chili."

"Love is a strong word," she mutters. "Chili and I are merely friends."

"Glad to hear it," I say, possessively wrapping an arm around her shoulders. "I'd hate to get jealous and throw down with a bowl of chili."

When Daisy laughs, her jitters disappear. She's suddenly okay, and I feel like a king for calming her.

Around us, my beloved redneck bar is filled with club members and their women. The older guys have old ladies. The younger guys bring current bed partners. I'm the only younger guy with an actual girlfriend. *As usual, I'm ahead of the curve.*

My dad and brother stand near the bar with Uncle Jude and a few men I don't recognize. Grabbing two bowls of chili, I hand one to Daisy as we remain distanced from the other people. She takes a few bites and then drinks a glass of water to deal with the heat. I finish my bowl quickly and promise to find her a milder chili.

When Mojo calls my name, I know private time is over. Sighing, I tell Daisy over the loud music, "Let's meet the family and make the formal introductions."

"Do I have to be friendly?"

"No. Do the shy thing, so people won't want to talk to us. I'm not searching for meaningful chats this evening."

Daisy grins at how her anti-social ways are helpful for once. I take her delicate hand in my rough one and walk to the bar top.

"Look at who honors us with his appearance," Mojo says, shaking his head as if I'm a shit for not being the first guy at the bar.

"Hey, Dad, where's your latest floozy?"

Dayton rolls his eyes at my comment, but Mojo is unfazed. "She's in the bathroom, making herself pretty."

"You know Daisy Crest," I casually announce as if my bringing a woman here is no big deal.

"How's your mom?" Mojo asks, and I pray he hasn't nailed Sally Slater.

"She's fine. Thanks."

"Good-looking women run in your family."

"I know," Daisy says, and I smile at how her tension makes her snippy. She's so fucking sexy in a bitchy mood. "Thank you."

"Do you like chili?" Dayton asks Daisy, and I frown at my brother's friendliness.

"Yes. Do you?"

"Fuck, yes."

"Harmony doesn't," Daisy says, arching an eyebrow. She's obviously challenging Dayton, who has spent years sniffing around the Lush Gardens Trailer Park in pursuit of one particular blonde.

"Don't care," Dayton says, taking a swig of beer. "Hey, bro, guess who this fella is."

I look at the man standing with Jude. Tall, blond, and lanky, he's got a familiar vibe, but I don't recognize him.

"Who?"

"This is my son, Jude Junior," Howler declares while throwing his arm around the grinning man's neck.

My uncle looks like a fucking loon, but everyone except me pretends to be thrilled with his ridiculous news. Jude acts as if he doesn't have an illegitimate son living in the same condo complex as Dayton and me. Hell, he probably has a dozen illegitimate kids around Tennessee. What the fuck is so great about this guy?

When I say nothing, Howler asks, "Worried about the competition?"

My temper gets the better of me. I always have trouble thinking of Bonn and Jude without getting riled up. While I ought to behave for Daisy's sake, I can't keep my damn mouth shut.

"You're fucking kidding. I've got three inches and probably fifty pounds on him. I'm a helluva lot prettier, too."

The guy laughs, but he's full of shit. "I'm JJ. I guess we're cousins. Don't see much of a resemblance."

I only frown at my father, who shrugs. I'm wondering who JJ's thug friends are when I catch one of them looking at Daisy.

"If you get tired of this sissy, you give me a call," says the dark-haired freak before giving Daisy a wink.

Not a thought crosses my mind before my hands reach for the fucker. My reaction is primal—kill the interloper, protect my woman, caveman shit. Nothing matters beyond him looking at Daisy.

The first punch knocks him back. The second sends him against a stool. Taking hold of his hair, I repeatedly slam his face against the bar top.

Smelling blood in the air, I also hear the shocked hollering of the men around me. Their hands dig into my arms, pulling me away from my victim. Shoving them off, I won't be denied. I want this piece of shit dead, so he can never look at Daisy again.

After too many men put all their efforts into yanking me back, I'm pried from the asshole's limp body. I still struggle against my club brothers, but they're too strong, and I'm soon pinned to the wall.

"Calm the fuck down, boy!" Mojo yells and then lowers his voice to add, "You did what needed to be done, but now you need to show you aren't a loose cannon. Bring it down, son."

118

My struggles ease until I go slack in their grip. I glance between my father's face and Dayton who restrains my right shoulder. He stares at me in horror, of course, but I don't care about his opinion.

Daisy stands off to the side with a few of the old ladies. Unlike the enraged men shocked by my behavior, the women laugh at the violence. They've learned to dismiss our aggressive natures. It's a joke to them. If they treated the violence as a real problem, they'd need to worry about their men never coming home.

"Let me up," I tell my father. "I want to check on Daisy."

"She's fine. The women will keep her busy."

"If you killed Lincoln, we could have a problem," Dayton says, stating the obvious.

"The guy came at me, and I defended myself. Problem fucking solved."

Mojo smiles at my answer, but Dayton continues to eyeball me.

"I'll check on the asshole. You stay here," Mojo says, patting my shoulder.

When my dad walks over to Howler and the other guys, I notice a few of the club brothers smirking. They don't care about an out-of-town fucker. I'm family while this Lincoln idiot isn't. Mojo still needs to pretend for Howler's sake.

Dayton punches my shoulder to get my attention. "You need to see a doctor about whatever the fuck has gone wrong with your fat head, brother."

"Why are you crying over some bitch making eyes at my woman?"

"Now, she's your woman?" Dayton asks, looking horrified. "You've been dating for a week."

"A man knows."

"Now, you're a man? You've acted like a childish fuck for your entire life."

"I still don't know what you're whining about."

Dayton leans in closer until I can smell the chili on his breath. "I know you, and this ain't you. You're laid-back about chicks. You think before you fucking act. Now, you're losing your shit when you ought to be focused on the bigger picture."

"What picture is that?"

Dayton leans in closer, forcing me to stare into a duplicate of my face. Even after all these years, I find myself shocked by how much we look alike. No facial scars or opposing cowlicks to tell us apart.

"Howler is acting like he's found his long-lost son," Dayton grumbles.

"Sure, but he's an idiot."

"Mojo and Howler built the Brotherhood together. The only reason our father is the president is that he married a Hallstead. Howler has as much claim to the club as Mojo does. That makes JJ an heir to the club, just like you and me. That asshole isn't showing up now for shits and giggles."

Even without glancing at JJ, I feel the fucker looking at me. "He's in for a rude awakening if he thinks he can steal what's ours."

"Are you sure because he's looking like a hardass with his own crew while you're looking like a spoiled brat throwing a tantrum over your new bitch."

"Don't call Daisy that, or I'll break your head open next, Dayton."

"That's what I'm talking about."

"You think taking JJ's shit would make me look like a better man? Are you fucking dense?"

Dayton backs off and shrugs. "I'm thinking about the big picture rather than this fucking second with these people. I'm thinking about what JJ is doing here now and what he has planned. You need to do the same, or you might not be our next president. Get it, pussy slave?"

"If need be, I'll finish JJ before he starts trouble for us."

"He might be thinking that about you."

Frowning darkly, I want to glance at JJ and size him up. He's likely still watching me, and I don't want the jackass knowing he's the topic of our conversation.

Dayton gives me another apathetic shrug. "I'm not saying I didn't enjoy watching you brain that fucker, but you gotta know how to pace yourself."

"I like when you pretend to be the smart brother."

Dayton shares my smile. "I might not be the serious one, but I have my big brass balls still firmly under my control. I wouldn't be surprised to learn Daisy's cats are chasing yours around her place."

"Do you think Daisy would freak out if I punched you in the face?"

"Oh, yeah, and we don't want her freaking out."

"No, we probably don't," I say, patting him hard on the shoulder.

Smiling, Dayton pounds me just as rough on the cheek. We eye one another, and I sense a wrestling match coming. Before I can tackle my brother, Daisy appears at my side.

"I'm not hungry for chili," she says in an oddly sing-song voice. "Can we pick up something else on the way to my place?"

Dayton grins and steps away from me. "She's savvy with the hints."

"We'll talk later," I promise him.

"Oh, no doubt about that."

Once Dayton is out of reach, I study Daisy. Her hazel eyes watch me as if not truly seeing me. She isn't dazed, just faking a helluva calm demeanor.

"We'll leave."

Though Daisy smiles, there's nothing warm about her expression. My girl is about to freak the fuck out, and I doubt a night of tasting my tongue will be enough to improve her mood. While I don't regret beating down the out-of-town fucker, I'll pay a price for my temper. I sense the one doling out the punishment will be this tiny, pissed woman who owns my heart.

TWENTY ONE - DAISY

All those stupid dreams in my head come in handy when I watch Camden nearly kill a man. Over the years, I've pretended to be so many different people. Now, I play the cool chick completely unfazed by psycho violence. *I'm chill, baby.*

Except I'm not chill. I'm freaking out, and I don't know how long I can keep up the lie. Around me, the club's old ladies joke about how their men are so rowdy. They're pretending, too. Better at the lies, they don't struggle against tears. Their hands don't shake so badly they need to shove them into their pockets. These women are aces at playing cool, and I do my best to keep up with their bullshit.

"Be cool," I mentally chant while they talk around me. "Be cool," I beg myself when I see the men drag the bloody guy outside. "Be cool," I still say in my head as Camden walks with me to the parking lot nearly a half hour later.

I finally stop playing cool when he cups my face with bloodied hands. Camden smiles as if this is any other day, and we're just any other people.

"What the heck was that?" I growl, failing to tame my temper. "You... I just don't even know what that was."

Camden gives me a frown as if I'm the one with the issues. "I thought it was pretty obvious. He made a move on you, and I made a move on him. That's how life works, babe."

"Don't 'babe' me. You nearly killed him."

"A guy in his line of work needs to learn how to walk off that shit."

Horrified, I remind him, "You're in that line of work, too. Should I expect someone to pound your face into a bar top like that?"

"They can try," Camden says with an arrogant smirk.

"Your male bravado doesn't impress me. You think it's sexy or cool or what-the-fuck-ever, but you sound like a

123

pissy child. You should know I'm not a thing you need to defend."

Camden glances around before taking me by the arm and maneuvering me away from the bar.

"Explain what you think happened in there. Because I don't think you get it."

Based on his expression, I wonder if I really am the screwed-up one. "Tell me."

"I plan to lead this club. Do you think I can have some fucking loser show up at my family's bar and make eyes at my girl? What does that say about me if I just shrug it off? I'll tell you."

Lowering his voice, he continues, "It says I'm weak and won't fight if someone tries to take my shit. This isn't about you, Daisy. This is about me preventing assholes from starting trouble. I make an example of that one guy and save myself from having to fight a dozen of them. Hell, I might have saved myself from fighting a fucking hundred. That's how Mojo and Howler gained power. They made a big show and scared off the pretenders. That's what I need to do now. This isn't about looking tough for you or showing off or whatever bullshit you have in your beautiful head."

"Oh," is all I can think to say.

Camden's angry expression fades. His hands cup my face again, and I still can't shake off how they turned violent so recently.

"If I take a stand now in a big way, I don't have to do it every day."

Feeling weak in this world of warriors, I just want to go home to my little trailer, cats, and life.

"I thought you were pissed because he was talking to me. I didn't want you freaking out on my account, but I never thought about it like you mean. People respond to fear and authority. I get it."

Camden's dark eyes study my face. "Do you really, or are you just saying that because I got angry with you?"

"Both."

"What happened in there was fucked up, and I didn't want shit to go down like that. I figured you'd meet my friends. They'd see how great you are. You'd see how the club life wasn't so scary. That all went the fuck out the window, and I'm worried you'll bolt."

Sighing unsteadily, I try to calm my nerves. "I'm sorry I thought you were freaking out over me. You've been weird about guys and interfering with my other dates. I assumed you were playing the possessive dick. The club stuff makes sense. It's smart for the long term. I want you to be smart because I want you to be safe."

Camden nods but says nothing. I study him for a long time while people walk past us. Something about Camden's behavior feels off, and I narrow my eyes.

"Did you attack him because you were feeling possessive? No bullshit."

"I answered that."

"Answer it again and look me in the eyes when you say the words." I widen my eyes and hardcore stare at him. "Say the words and don't lie."

Camden leans down and stares into my eyes. "You are mine. The club is mine. That guy isn't mine. I did what I had to."

"You won't freak out if some guy at the movie theater or the grocery store says hello to me, right?"

"Of course, I won't freak out," Camden says, shoving his hands in his pockets. "Will I tell this hypothetical piece of shit to mind his fucking business and stay away from my woman? Fucking-A, I will, but there won't be any freaking out."

"Later, when I'm home alone, I'm planning to cry into my pillow about how scared I was in there. Until then, I'm keeping my shit undercover. Did I do good?"

"So good," he says, softly kissing me.

"I wanted to run when you grabbed him."

"I know, but you didn't."

"You were calm, and then you were—"

125

Camden waits for me to finish, but I can't. I don't know what word fits what I saw in him when he attacked the guy. *Ferocious. Unhinged. Terrifying.* None of those words feel accurate when thinking about a man I know is capable of such tenderness and humor. Camden isn't a monster or a thug. He's more, better, perfect. But he also trashed another human being in less than a minute.

"I want to go home," I say, feeling exhausted. "Is that okay?"

"Are you running away?"

"If I were, I'd knock you down, steal your keys, drive Shasta to my place, and lock the door on you. Instead, I'm kindly asking for you to take me home."

Camden leans down and kisses my cheek. "I'd like to see you knock me down. I bet you're sneaky in a fight."

"No, I'm very fair and high-minded. I'd never scratch your eyes out or bite."

Camden smiles, but I see him intensely studying me. He wants reassurance. I want it too. Neither of us will get any tonight. Camden drives me home, where he parks and follows me to the trailer.

"Bye," I say, stretching up to kiss him.

Camden gives me his "man knows best" expression. "No, 'bye.' I'm staying the night."

"Why?"

"I'm too emotional to drive home. Wouldn't be safe."

I place my hands on his hard chest and push. "I think I'm starting my period. You should go."

"I'll rub your tummy."

"I have gas."

Camden only smiles. "After chili, gas is gonna happen. Let's go inside and watch TV and fart."

"I want to be alone," I mutter, exasperated by how he always gets his way.

"No."

"No?"

"I'm your man, and I don't want to be alone tonight. You have to baby me."

"Is that right?" I ask, grinning despite my irritation. "What if I say no?"

"I'll sit out here and howl at the moon."

"There are a few howling cats that'll keep you company."

"Should I beg?" he asks, pressing a hand against my door so I can't open it.

"Don't."

"Why are you acting icy with me?"

Unable to believe this is a real question, I only say, "I'm in a bad mood."

"So?"

"So, I want to be alone."

"And I *don't* want to be alone. Why should you win?"

"Why should you win?"

"Because I'd let you win if you were sad and needed to cuddle."

"This is bullshit," I complain. "How can I say no when you act pathetic?"

"You can't," Camden murmurs, kissing the top of my head while taking my keys to unlock the trailer's front door. "I promise not to gloat."

Camden walks into my place, and I can only follow him. He kicks off his boots and walks to my bathroom. I hear him washing up and figure he's getting rid of the guy's blood.

Remaining in the kitchen, I think of how quickly Camden went from easy-going to ruthless. I know I should fear him, but I'm mostly afraid for him. His life is frigging scary.

"You're tense," Camden says, stretching out on my tiny couch. "Let me massage your shoulders and breasts. I bet your inner thighs need attention, too."

"No."

127

Camden turns on the TV, flips around, and stops on a "King of the Hill" rerun. "Want to laugh at Texan cartoon people?"

"No."

"Want me to go down on you?" he asks, wiggling his eyebrows.

"Maybe," I mumble, unsure if there's ever a reason to turn down something that feels so good.

Camden grins and pats the couch. "Come here."

"No."

"You like that word."

"It makes me feel powerful."

"When you suck on my tongue, you're a dominant warrior princess. Now come over here and embrace your power."

I walk to the couch and straddle him, but my lips don't find his. I rest my head against his shoulder and grip his shirt. "Don't talk."

Camden wraps his arms around me, and we remain that way through the rest of the episode and into a new one. I finally kiss him and embrace my warrior princess power. He rewards me with a little downtown action.

We don't talk about our time at Salty Peanuts except later when he rips one loud enough to startle the cats out of the bedroom. Laughing, I pretend like the Brotherhood's old ladies pretend when reality becomes too ugly to face.

TWENTY TWO - CAMDEN

For the first time since setting my sights on Daisy, I wonder if I've made a mistake. I'm taken aback by her terrified expression in the parking lot. Daisy looks at me as if I'm a psycho, and she needs to make a run for safety.

Hours after I beat down what's his face, she remains tense and even wants me to sleep at my place for the night. I refuse, of course. Daisy is mine, and I won't let a little thing like her fear get in our way.

We climb into bed around eleven, and Daisy pretends to sleep. I rest next to her, listening to the trailer park noises. My condo is so quiet, and I can't relax with the racket here. At least, not without a good vigorous fuck first.

"I'm lonely," I murmur, tugging at her nightgown.

"Is that code for horny?"

"It's code for I want you naked riding my cock."

"I'm not in the mood."

"I could help you get in the mood."

"Nope. I'm happy the way I am."

I realize going down on her won't move things into the fucking realm. Instead, I'll likely satisfy her while I get stuck with a raging hard-on.

"What am I supposed to do with this?" I ask, poking her with my erection.

"You own two hands. Have at it."

Grinning in the dark, I lean back on the bed and squirm out of my boxers. This proves to be a tricky feat, considering how small everything is in the trailer. I nearly kick a cat at one point, and I'm fairly sure I bump Daisy with my ass. She says nothing, and I realize she isn't playing the silent treatment. She's fully entrenched in it.

I spit in my palm and fist my disappointed cock. Stroking it, I watch Daisy and imagine her hand doing the loving.

Slowly massaging my cock, I murmur, "So beautiful. Yes, Daisy, don't stop."

"Really?" she grumbles, turning over to frown at me. "I said no."

"Shh, I'm trying to concentrate."

"Stop talking while you do that."

"Hush or I'll give you the play-by-play in my head of you sucking me off."

Daisy glares at me. While I can't see her full fury in the dark room, I sure as fuck can feel it.

"You're an asshole," she says, sitting up and pulling off her nightgown.

"What are you doing? I don't need any pity fucks," I ask, fighting laughter.

"Shut up," she says in a weird voice, and I realize she's trying not to laugh, too. "First, you turn me on. Now, you want to play hard to get? No way, buddy."

"Well, okay," I say, resting my arms behind my head and watching her climb over me. "I don't want to be a tease."

"Asshole."

"What? I can't hear you over my cock's applause."

Daisy leans forward and kisses me. I sense none of her irritation. Once her fingers wrap around my cock and slide it along the folds of her pussy, I don't feel a fucking thing outside of pleasure.

My fingers travel up the soft skin on her arms before dipping down to where her breasts crave my touch. Pinching her nipples between my knuckles, I cup her mounds of flesh.

"Daisy, don't be angry," I whisper as she strokes my cock with her pussy. "A man needs to protect what's his, or else people will take it away. I can't lose you again."

Even in the dark, I see the change in Daisy's expression. She needs to be angry because the violence scares her. I know how much rage can soothe less helpful feelings like fear and loss. My words touch her, and I know she understands me a little bit better tonight than she did the day before.

A smile crosses her face, and she presses the head of my cock inside her. Despite the thorough fucking I gave Daisy the night before, she still needs to wiggle and work to take my size. I watch her but don't help. Her confidence in bed can't come from me, controlling her like a master with his doll. She needs to know what she wants and learn to take it.

The next morning, I wake up with a cat sleeping between my legs and one perched on Daisy's head. I frown at the latter cat staring at me with the indifferent gaze of an alpha. I admire his arrogance but still swat him off her.

Daisy opens her eyes and stares at me. She's clearly been awake for a while, meaning the cat on her head was a conscious choice.

"How are you feeling?" I ask.

"I've decided to pretend I view last night's brutality as a turn on."

"Smart cookie."

"Is there anything you'll ever change for me?"

"I've already changed plenty. Like the cats climbing on me all night would have been a no-go for any other chick. I also slept over, and I don't like sleeping at other people's places."

"Anything else?"

"Nope. Wait, I'm chasing you, and I'd never do that for another woman."

Daisy studies me before nodding and sitting up in bed. "I'm choosing to believe we're on equal footing."

When she gets up, I follow her, but she hides in the bathroom before I get a kiss. "Equal footing is overrated," I say through the door.

"Probably. I'm rarely in charge, but I still don't like feeling as if I don't have a choice."

The toilet flushes, and I hear the water running. She brushes her teeth and washes her face before opening the door and smiling at me.

"You're sexy as hell, but I can't choose to embrace morning breath," she says and gestures at the sink. "I put a toothbrush out for you."

"Yes, ma'am."

"I'm in charge!" she cries, scooting past me. "It feels great but a little overwhelming."

"No worries," I say, walking into the bathroom while she heads to the kitchen. "You won't be in charge for long."

I piss and then brush my teeth. The bathroom feels too small for my build. The entire trailer makes me duck even when there's space.

In the kitchen, Daisy pours cups of coffee, but I'm more interested in her.

"Let's sleep at my place tonight," I say, wrapping her in my arms.

Daisy's kisses are hot, and I suspect she really has chosen to embrace last night's violence. I protected what's mine, and she approves of my possessive nature. At least, that's what I get from our wild kiss and her roving hands.

Before we end up back in bed, Daisy's alarm goes off. Now, I'm stuck with a painful pair of blue balls as I drop her off at work. Based on her expression when we part, she's nursing damp panties. Our mutual suffering offers me confidence about our future.

Those blue balls are nothing compared to the pain of knowing I have to dump the JJ news on Bonn. Better he learns it from me than someone else, but I still don't feel like being the guy to ruin his day.

Bonn mainly works in construction but picks up shifts as a pizza delivery man during the off-seasons. Somehow, he makes enough to pay for a condo in our building. If he didn't have the money to live here, I'd give it to him. He's a great guy and has always had my back. He remains loyal to the Rutgers family, even if it rarely repays the favor.

His single mom's only support when Bonn was growing up came from the Hallstead women. They sent checks but refused to include him in family events. After all, Jude has plenty of bastards running around, and no one wants them all showing up for Christmas.

I catch up to my cousin as he cleans out his used SUV. The once messy teenager grew into a clean freak. Having a kid changes people, Bonn often says. I know he wishes he changed before Chevelle was born, so he'd still have Ruby. Instead, he's a single dad working his ass off to make his kid proud.

"Heard you freaked out on some guy," Bonn says, dumping trash from his SUV. "Dayton claims you fight like a little bitch, and I should teach you how to be a man."

"He's a classy fucking dickhead, ain't it?" I grumble, ready to glue my brother's ass closed. "Did he say anything else about last night?"

"That you brought Daisy to the chili thing and called her your woman. He was rather irritated about that."

"Yeah, Dayton is anti-commitment lately."

Bonn pushes his dark hair out of his eyes and smiles at me. "What did Daisy think of your freak out?"

"She thought I was sexy," I say, skipping the part where she wanted space. "The guy I banged up was from out of town. He apparently works with your half-brother."

"Which half-brother would that be?"

"A new one who calls himself JJ."

Bonn shrugs like he doesn't care and returns to cleaning. "Howler has plenty of kids, Camden. I'm not sure why you think I should reach for the Kleenex over this one."

"Howler brought him to the club and was making a big deal out of JJ."

"The guy probably kissed the old man's ass. Doesn't take much to get on his good side," he says and then adds, "Doesn't take much to get on his bad side, either."

"This guy seems like he plans to hang around in Hickory Creek."

"So?" Bonn asks, giving me a frown.

"So, nothing. I just thought I'd tell you."

"You know I don't care about club business, and I'm long past giving a shit about Howler throwing me any hugs and kisses. Don't worry about it, Cam."

Nodding, I lean against his SUV. "Do you think I'm moving too fast with Daisy?"

"No," he says, reaching into the SUV to grab a scrap of paper. "Daisy overthinks shit. The longer you let her think, the more likely she'll talk herself out of getting serious. Not just with you but with any guy. The chick tends to cock block herself in life."

"There's something special about Daisy. Giving her up isn't an option."

"Then don't," Bonn says and shuts the SUV door. "Dayton makes shit too complicated. I think he's overcompensating for being a dumbass for most of his life, but he now overthinks things like Daisy. Don't be like them. Just decide Daisy is yours and keep her. She'll either say yes or no. Just don't wait around for her to make big moves, or you'll never get anywhere. Everyone has weaknesses, and that's hers."

"That's her only weakness. I swear she even makes me like her cats."

"Love will change your outlook, man," he says, giving me a pat on the shoulder before he heads inside.

Smiling, I roll the word "love" around in my head. I feel it for my family and the club, sure. But this thing with Daisy is deeper, more painful. She makes me doubt myself, and no one is a bigger fan of the Cam Man than me.

TWENTY THREE - DAISY

I've dreaded this conversation since Camden and I began spending every night together. He wants to be with me, and I love his company, but Friday nights aren't negotiable. I suspect Camden will see the issue differently. While he's accustomed to winning everything he wants, I need to learn how to occasionally be triumphant.

"Tomorrow night, let's head out to the Hillside Steakhouse. On the weekends, they serve special French fries," he says while we sit in my trailer and relax in our post-coital bliss.

"I can't go out on Fridays," I nearly whisper. "I made an exception last Friday since we'd just started dating. But from now on, I need my Fridays to myself."

Camden's demeanor changes immediately. His body goes tense next to me on the couch, and he hits the DVD pause button. "Why?"

"I have plans with my sisters on Fridays."

"What kind of plans?"

Shrugging, I stare at the frozen TV screen. "The kind that doesn't involve you."

"I don't know what that means. Sounds wrong somehow for the world not to revolve around me. Are you sure this is kosher, babe?"

"Don't make an issue out of it," I say, hitting play on the remote.

The movie "Old Boy" will need to wait once Camden pauses it again. "Wouldn't dream of making an issue out of something so insignificant. Now, why don't you tell me what you do on Fridays with your sisters?"

I glance at him and shrug. "Girl shit."

"I have no sisters, so throw me a bone and explain what 'girl shit' means."

Sighing, I lean back on the couch and pet Hong Kong resting in my lap. "We talk about our periods and giving birth and the best tampons. That sort of thing."

"Every Friday?" he mutters, turning off the TV as if making a point that we don't get to watch the Korean thriller unless I bow to his will.

"Yes."

"You're lying about something. Fess up."

Standing, I walk to my stereo and turn on a CD. I bob my head to the sounds of the Go-Go's singing "Head Over Heels." Camden remains on the couch where I left him. He glances at the music and then at me. I know he's plotting to get his way.

So far, I haven't figured out how to beat him in a disagreement of any kind. If he wants something, we do it. Even bitching and struggling, I always end up relenting under the power of Camden's personality. There must be a way to defeat the spoiled sex god.

"What time do you and the girls get together to talk about tampons?" he asks, finally joining me in the kitchen where I dodge his groping hands.

"Why?"

"I realize I'm not hip to the problems of today's ladies. If I sat in with you girls, I might learn a thing or two about how to treat the fairer sex."

"No."

"How come? Don't you want me to respect chicks more?"

"If you want to get in touch with your feelings, watch Oprah."

"I don't think she's on TV anymore."

Patting his cheek, I sigh. "It makes me sad for you to know that."

"What are you hiding?" he asks, trapping me in a kitchen corner. "What happens on Fridays?"

"I told you."

"You're lying, Bourbon Babe. I know you are because you're a horrible liar. My theory is you can actually lie well but choose to do a shitty job with me because you want me to know the truth."

"I really, really don't."

Camden keeps me blocked in the corner. His gaze only leaves mine for long enough to glance down at Seoul scenting our legs before heading to the couch. I wish I could sneak away as quickly as the cat.

"What do you do on Fridays?" Camden asks again.

"What do you think we do?"

"I don't know, but it's not tampon talk."

"We have been known to discuss tampons on occasion."

"So, what do you do on Fridays?"

Shrugging, I try to weasel my way past him. He shifts his hip and blocks me.

"Camden, you're an ass."

"I'm only worried about you. What if you're addicted to gambling or porn? I'll need to help you kick the habit by gambling or watching porn with you."

"I'm not addicted to anything except maybe Twix or possibly hamburgers."

"And me, right?" he asks, nudging his knee between my legs. "I need you to be addicted to me. I'm an insecure douche that way."

"Yes, I'm addicted to you," I say, smiling reluctantly.

"Then, tell me what you do on Fridays."

"Why?"

"Why not? The more you hold out, the more I want to know the answer."

"You keep your secrets. Why can't I have mine?"

"I have no secrets. I only have things I don't tell you because I know you don't want to know. This Friday night thing is something I want to know."

I glare up at Camden, who smiles down at me. We play the staring game for a long minute. I nearly sneak past him when he's distracted by a song on the stereo. Before I can dodge him, he wraps an arm around my shoulders and leads me to the couch.

"What in the hell are you listening to?" he asks.

"That's the Pet Shop Boys," I mutter, stuck on his lap. When he only stares at me, I elaborate, "They were big in the 1980s."

"You picked the wrong decade to get moist over, babe. The 1970s are better. The music was outstanding, and so were the films. What did the '80s give us besides big hair and bad synthesizers?"

"I think I might have to break up with you now."

"Nope. So, what happens on Fridays?" he asks, refusing to give up.

"We listen to 1980s music."

"Why would that be a secret? Is it because you know the music is frigging awful?" he teases, poking my chest before his fingers decide to caress my soft nipple.

Leaning into his touch, I remind him, "The '70s had bell-bottoms, shag carpet, and porn mustaches."

"Like I said, it was the best. So, what happens on Fridays?"

"You're fucking annoying when you nag."

"Well, I want to know, and you're going to tell me. For whatever reason, you make me nag before you give in. If anyone's to blame for my annoying fucking behavior, it's you. I forgive you, though."

Rolling my eyes, I tug free of him and sit on the other end of the couch. "We do karaoke in Ruby's trailer."

Camden studies me. "Why would you hide that from me?"

"It's our private business."

"You're a bad singer, aren't you?" he says, chuckling. "No worries. I'm still addicted to you."

I cross my arms and sigh. "Nagging is an awful habit."

"It truly is. You should stop forcing me to stoop that low."

"Stop blaming me for your crap."

Smiling, he reaches out and caresses my cheek. "Can I listen to you sing?"

"This is why I didn't tell you," I say, jumping up and walking to the kitchen. "Karaoke is my private thing with my sisters, so, no, you cannot come and listen."

"Why is it private? How bad can you be?"

"It's not about that. It's that we get to be together and do our thing, and no one bothers us."

"What about Chevelle and Harmony's kid?"

"They stay at my mom's place overnight."

Following me to the kitchen, Camden pins me to the fridge. "Do you drink?"

"Yes."

"It's just you, Ruby, and Harmony?"

"Yes."

Camden steps back and nods. "I will allow this."

"You're pissing me off."

"Think about it from my point of view. I've never committed to a woman like I'm committed to you. It's important to me for you to be safe and happy."

"Well, the safe part you have down, but you're not firing on all cylinders with the happy part."

"You're too sensitive."

"No, I like to do what I like to do."

"Yes, but that was when you were one person. Now you're part of a couple, so it matters what we both want."

"Can I tell you what to do?"

Camden smirks. "Sure."

"Will you listen?"

"Listen? Yes. Obey? Maybe. It'll depend."

"So, I don't have to obey you, then?"

"No," he says, crossing his arms. "If you can devise a way to win an argument, I'll bow to your will."

"Once I find a way to win, you'll pay for all your nagging, Camden Cheesestick Rutgers."

"It's sexy when you growl my name like that. You sound the same way when I make you come."

Rolling my eyes, I hurry away from him. He's winning like he always does. I want him so much, but I need alone time, too. Well, not alone time as much as sister time.

"Is the karaoke machine here?" he asks, picking me up and carrying me to the couch. "I'll sing you some Skynyrd, so you'll know real music."

"It belongs to Ruby."

"I wouldn't think her the karaoke type."

"She won it in her work's Christmas party raffle when she was still bartending. We tried it and had fun. Now it's *our* thing," I say, hoping he won't show up and force us to let him join in.

"What do you sing? Is it this crap?"

I caress the dark hairs poking from his ripped black T-shirt. "You need to stop talking shit about my music."

"Sorry, but I calls them like I sees them."

"KISS sucks."

"Careful," he says, tugging at my nipple through my bra.

"I hate Led Zeppelin."

Narrowing his eyes, he pinches the nipple. "You keep that up and no oral sex for you, young lady."

"Pink Floyd gives me diarrhea," I announce, trying not to laugh.

"Woman," he growls.

"The Cure could kick Deep Purple's ass."

"I must make you shut up."

Kissing me, Camden refuses to let me speak for the rest of the night. When I talk shit about the Rolling Stones while he eats me out, Camden sticks his finger in my mouth and orders me to suck it.

Later, I mention The Who sounds like a colostomy, and he fills my mouth with cock. I'm laughing so hard at his reaction I nearly choke. We find a fun way to trash each other's music, but I'm still at a loss on how to win an argument against my nagging Viking.

TWENTY FOUR - CAMDEN

Missing Daisy on her karaoke night, I don't know what to do with myself. I consider hanging out with Dayton, but he's too busy chasing tail. Knowing Bonn is working, I realize I need more damn friends. The other club guys are with their wives, girlfriends, or sluts on the side. I can sit alone at home, or I can hang out with my mom. Like a good mama's boy, I choose the latter.

Clara is in the kitchen when I arrive. I see Hudson with his dad, Erik, in the backyard. Dressed in fatigues, they look ready to invade Baghdad. I don't bother them. Instead, I sit at the kitchen island where Clara cuts lemons.

"Have you spoken to your dad about De Campo's Pizza Shop?" she immediately asks.

"He's thinking about it."

"What's that mean?"

"He doesn't want to do something to piss you off, but he can't look weak. So, he's pretending to think about it first. De Campo should be fine."

Clara walks over and gives my cheek a motherly peck. "You're a good boy."

"I reminded him how Common Bend has a handful of strip clubs, and he still has his eye on the town."

"Taking Common Bend is ridiculous, but your father is an emotional man at times."

"He lost the town to the Reapers, and he thinks taking it back fixes a past humiliation."

"Men and their egos," Mom says, walking to the fridge.

"Have you heard about Jude's newest bastard?"

"Yes. Jude brought him by Alice's house the other night."

As the town sheriff, my aunt has a nose for bullshitters. "What did she think of him?"

"She called him Eddie Haskell."

"Who's that?"

Clara sighs. "Kids today have no idea what they're missing."

"I still don't know who that is."

"He's a kiss-ass character on the show 'Leave It to Beaver.'"

"Sounds about right. What did you think?"

"I thought my brother was acting like a damn fool, tripping over himself to show off some kid claiming to be his."

"Claiming?"

"Jude swears there's a DNA test to prove it, but I don't know if I believe everything is on the up-and-up. Jude has other kids, but this one is making him behave like a clown."

"The guy bugs me. I'd get rid of him if I could."

Clara pats my arm. "But you can't. Not without stirring up a hornet's nest in the club."

"It's bullshit how JJ gets the welcome mat while Bonn is treated like a frigging ghost."

"JJ takes after Jude while Bonn's never had a taste for the lifestyle."

I think about my cousin working hard to do right by his kid. He'd be more of an asset to the club than an out-of-town thug like JJ. Of course, Bonn doesn't want to join the Brotherhood.

"Do you think JJ could work his way into the club?" I ask my mother rather than my father and brother, who'd know the answer.

"Are you worried about your birthright?" she asks, squeezing lemons into a pitcher. "Think the newcomer will steal your crown?"

I narrow my eyes and glare at Clara, but she only smiles. "Where's that coming from?"

"Aunt Alice said something like that after meeting JJ."

"What do you think?"

"You ought to worry about Dayton. He's been odd lately. Mojo called Dayton at four in the morning to pick him up condoms so he could nail biker groupies. Your brother ran out and did it. I don't like how his lips are too firmly attached to Mojo's butt lately."

"He's been weird about Daisy and me, too."

Grinning, Clara stops messing with her lemonade. "How are things going with Miss Crest?"

"Daisy is mine, and I'm keeping her. If anyone fucks that up, I'll rip their fucking heads off."

"Well, that clears that up."

Crossing my arms tightly, I'm aching for a fight. I miss Daisy and talking about her rubs salt in the wound.

"Mojo and Dayton act as if my relationship with Daisy makes me weak. They think they can shame me into dumping her. At this point, I'm ready to hurt anyone who so much as hints they'll stand in our way."

"Your dad doesn't want to give up the club, but he knows he can't run it much longer. When a man gets too old, enemies want to fight him. Mojo can still do what needs to be done, but fighting can be messy. If he leaves the club to you soon, he ensures it remains strong. His ego is holding him back. That and Jude's new heir makes your path less certain."

"He better not hang on for too long. I'd hate to organize a fucking coup against my own dad, but the club is more than one man and his ego."

Clara studies me with brightly curious eyes. "Would you do that?"

"He and Howler waste time on bullshit and ignore real opportunities. They cling to their old school thinking, but the world has moved on, and our enemies already adjusted. We need to do the same."

"It's true they still obsess over Common Bend. I don't know why they'd want such a dump."

"Even after all these damn years, they're nursing a grudge. It's like the bitches from high school starting rumors about their old enemies. They ought to let the shit go and move on, but they won't. Howler wants Common Bend, and Dad is convinced their moment will arrive. They ought to be looking to grab territory south from here, not fighting over a shithole I doubt the Reapers even want anymore."

"You're going to make a great leader."

"Daisy hasn't made me soft. It's gotten me focused," I say, sounding angrier than I intend.

"You don't have to convince me."

"You still need convincing about her and me. I see it on your face."

Clara pours a glass of lemonade and sets the pitcher in the fridge. She's taking her time before getting to her point.

"She isn't the type of woman to do well in your lifestyle."

"What type of woman is that?"

"Tough. I couldn't handle it. I thought I was strong, but the life wore me down."

"Daisy isn't you."

"No, she isn't. She grew up in the trailer park, and maybe that makes her stronger than she seems. Still, you asked my opinion, and I gave it to you."

"I'm not giving her up."

"I'm not asking you to."

"You never would. You'd just disapprove until I give in."

Clara smirks. "Oh, that I would, but you're not a love-struck teenager conned by a harlot. You're a grown man, and what I know about Daisy makes me think you call the shots. I trust your judgment."

I'm happy with my mother's words at first. We talk about her upcoming summer travel plans, and I feel confident that she understands my feelings for Daisy. Except that around ten minutes into her Bahamas details, I realize she hasn't asked to meet my woman. Mojo invited Daisy to the chili cook-off so he could size her up. Clara hasn't made any such offers, and I lose interest in listening to her bikini worries.

"What's the matter?" she asks when I get up and begin pacing.

144

"Normally, I'd spend the evening with Daisy."

Clara studies me, and I imagine her thinking ugly shit about my woman. "Why not train with Hudson and Erik? They're working with night goggles in the field."

"I wouldn't mind shooting some shit," I admit. "Thanks."

My mother knows I'm pissed. She's a smart chick and reads people well. I also read people pretty well. She thinks I'm enjoying a fling. I suspect her view of Daisy is tainted by her past with Sally Slater. Mustang Sally is known for her love of booze, dancing, and cards. Her attempts at commitment, on the other hand, have proven less successful. Same with Ruby and Harmony, so Clara wants to lump Daisy into the "unlucky in love" category.

I plan to prove my mother wrong.

TWENTY FIVE - DAISY

Pizza is an old lover I know is no good for me yet never leaves me unsatisfied. I inhale the scent of the delivery boxes, making Ruby laugh. Harmony sets out the paper plates and searches the pizzas for her veggie one. My sister isn't a vegetarian, but she doesn't like meat on her pizza. I don't know if she was dropped on her head as a baby. However, this would explain many of her quirkier qualities, such as her belief in the Mothman.

"I've missed you so much," I whisper to the first slice.

The pizza rewards me with hot, zesty goodness and a hint of heat from the sausage. I eat the first slice in a euphoric state. I'm even a little aroused. Ugh, I wish I hadn't asked for the entire night off from Camden.

"Someone misses her man," Ruby says, patting my head before flopping on the couch next to Harmony.

I study my sisters and notice once again how they share a bond I can't experience. Call it the "Lush Gardens Trailer Park Mommy Club" or just the bond between two women who've pushed a human being out of their crotches. I wonder if I'll get to join their crew once I have a kid.

The moment I imagine having a baby, I miss Camden. Who knows if he considers me baby mama material? But I'm definitely interested in creating a smaller version of my Viking. Even my tender vagina, still throbbing from our goodbye fuck, agrees with the idea of making a Camden Junior.

"Things are good with the lesser Rutgers boy?" Harmony asks me.

"Dayton is a poor man's version of Camden."

"Okay, sure, whatever you need to tell yourself, Bourbon Butt."

Rolling my eyes, I wish I hadn't shared Camden's nickname for me. Harmony giggles at my expression.

"I adore Camden," I announce. "I dig him inside and out. He's perfect. So, yeah, things are exquisite."

"I'm surprised he allowed you to spend the night without him."

"I have my skills."

"You begged, didn't you?" Ruby deadpans.

They laugh at my expression.

"I need to get the upper hand with these arguments with him. He nags and flirts and nags and won't give up until I give in."

"Flash a boob," Harmony suggests. "Dayton once told me his brother was a boob man while he was an ass man."

"Why would he tell you that?"

"It was back when I was waitressing, and he was trying to annoy me."

"Someone has a crush."

Harmony waves her hand dismissively. "While I've considered banging one out with Dayton and getting the urge out of our systems, I worry it might be too good, and I'd become addicted to Little Dayton. I can't deal with that in my life."

"Little Dayton," I snort.

"I also worry the sex would be awful, and my fantasy will be ruined."

Ruby smiles at our sister. "You've never gotten properly laid, so I can imagine how disappointed a bad fuck with Dayton would be."

Harmony nods. "I always screw men based on their personalities. Who'd think that leads to bad sex? Shouldn't I be rewarded with awesome sex for giving a nerd a break?"

"If there were any fairness in the world, you would," I mumble with a mouthful of pizza.

"Since Keanu, my vagina cringes at the thought of sex. No way do I want to get anywhere near Dayton's likely not little Little Dayton."

"Based on my knowledge of Little Camden, you've made a sane decision."

Ruby stares at me for a long time. "Tell me one negative thing about Camden. If it's lust, you won't see anything bad in him. If it's real, you can name at least one flaw."

"He has horrible taste in music. Oh, in fact, he actually said the Beastie Boys' music sounded like noise. Uh, yeah, right."

My sisters shake their heads, and Ruby says, "I knew there had to be a downside to all his hotness. Now, I know it."

"He doesn't even like 'Sabotage,' for goodness' sake. I didn't know how to respond to that. I just ended up having sex with him so he'd stop talking."

Laughing, my sisters give me a thumbs-up. I realize Harmony's suggestion about flashing a boob might work on Camden. Laser-focused, he always gets quiet whenever sex is on the table.

"We should put 'Sabotage' on the playlist tonight," Harmony suggests.

"What else are we doing?"

"'Vacation' in honor of Chevelle starting spring break plus 'Devil Inside' from INXS. I heard that one on the radio the other day and realized we've never sung it."

"How about 'Do You Really Want to Hurt Me'?" Harmony suggests.

Ruby rolls her eyes, even while nodding. Our little sister is obsessed with the Culture Club song ever since seeing "The Wedding Singer." While I feel no Adam Sandler movie should change someone's world views, few people are like Harmony.

Despite missing Camden, I enjoy the time alone with my sisters. No kids to worry over. No work to bitch about. We're young and free during our karaoke nights. Ruby lets go of her anger at the only man she's loved and belts out the songs they once enjoyed together. That usually means at least one tune by Bad English or John Waite.

In fact, after we nearly injure ourselves singing and jumping around to "Sabotage," Ruby insists on "Change" from Waite. Harmony and I hum in the background while my older sister sings her heart out.

What might seem silly to Camden—or anyone watching us dance—is how we release a week's worth of pent-up negativity. Life's disappointments wash away by the time we reach the final song of every karaoke night. The Outfield's "Your Love" is usually sung while we rest on the floor, exhausted from too much laughing and bad dance moves.

Tonight is no different. If Camden ever witnessed the sheer level of utter lameness I exude on karaoke nights, I doubt he'd get so laser-focused on sex. However, I never intend to test this theory.

TWENTY SIX - CAMDEN

Hudson's dad is a retired Delta Force operator who thinks the world will end tomorrow or the next day or at some point very soon. Erik isn't a fringe guy in most ways, but he trains as if the apocalypse is nigh.

The upside to his oddness is Hudson knows his way around weapons. At sixteen, he's better with rifles than I'll ever be. Stealthy like one of Daisy's cats before it trips me, my little brother sneaks around without even trying.

While Clara gossips on the phone with her sisters, I get dressed in fatigues. I even apply face paint, so I won't feel left out with Hudson and Erik. They're waiting for me outside, where next to the fenced yard is an obstacle course.

Hudson looks like a soldier when he moves through the darkness. I try to keep up, but he's smaller and disappears quickly. I hear Erik a few times when his footsteps land on dry leaves. Otherwise, I'm on my own.

I move around the various obstacles, climbing rope nets, crawling through a pipe tunnel, and balancing on a plank across a muddy hole. I take shots at targets scattered through the course. At first, I feel silly for needing this distraction just because Daisy can't entertain me for one fucking night.

When I think of JJ and his crew in Hickory Creek, my efforts take on more importance. I imagine I'm hunting them in the darkness. They're threats, and I'm the only one willing to put them down. My shots sharpen. My movements speed up. My instincts strengthen. Soon, I have a rhythm I keep until an hour later when I catch up to father and son taking a water break.

"You do this every Friday?" I ask Erik after sitting on a tree stump next to them.

"I'm keeping Hudson busy, so he doesn't think with his dick."

My brother shows no reaction. The kid is a fucking cipher most days. I can't even remember the last time we shared a conversation where I didn't wonder what he was hiding.

"Daisy has this thing she does on Fridays with her sisters. If it's okay with you, I'd like to train here those nights."

"The more, the merrier," Erik says, and I think he just told me he loves me in Erik-speak.

Hudson stands up like a dog catching a scent. His gaze searches the night. Erik doesn't seem worried, so I finish my water.

"I'm gonna take a piss before we start up again," I announce when they remain silent.

Still watchful, Hudson possesses his dad's odd nature. Dayton is another Mojo, leaving me the only son to take after Clara.

No wonder she loves me the best.

TWENTY SEVEN - DAISY

My dad isn't a hotshot lawyer. His tiny office is located between a tanning salon and a Subway in a shopping strip near Hickory Creek's border with Common Bend. His clients are slip and falls, nasty divorces, custody fights, and the occasional malpractice suit. His dream is to organize a class-action lawsuit against a big company. *This is seriously his only dream.*

Until the magical class action appears, Dad lives comfortably in a ranch-style house in a subdivision in a better part of Common Bend. He calls Hickory Creek Township a shithole, but I prefer it any day to the chaotic town he claims is on the rise.

While Ollie Crest isn't a bad father, he isn't someone I look up to. I can't imagine this info would come as a surprise to him or anyone else. He simply exists most days while my mom acts as if every day is a frigging party. I've seen her wake up with a smile on her face. I've also seen my father go all day without smiling. So, no, he isn't my role model.

I still drop by his office once a month to have lunch and talk like friends, even though we share nothing in common besides a last name and DNA.

We sit down at Subway with our sandwiches and struggle to keep up the conversation. I know many people think my father never remarried because he's still hung up on Sally. In reality, he lacks the self-care to draw any woman he'd find worthy of his time.

Rather than embrace his balding head and shave it like a lot of men do these days, Ollie pretends no one can tell he has a comb-over. His teeth are brownish from too little care and too many cigarettes. He buys suits off the rack that never fit him correctly. He has a white boy's flat ass and a middle-aged white man's gut. If he put half of the effort into his appearance as he does into his yard, I suspect he'd have a wife and better clientele. Even poor people don't want a lawyer who dresses like a hobo.

"I heard about a translation job in Nashville," Ollie says after we've bored each other with weather talk for long enough. "It's at the firm of a buddy of mine from law school."

Ollie hands me his buddy's card, and I look at the information. I like the idea of working as a translator but don't like owning my father anything. My mom says he's petty. I've rarely seen this quality in him, but he *is* a lawyer.

"Thanks."

"If you're working in downtown Nashville, you won't have time to date."

"How do you figure?"

"The drive will take a good hour."

Frowning, I know Ollie is talking around the Camden conversation. "My man is patient," I lie. "He can come over after I get home."

"So, you're dating the Rutgers kid?"

"Yes, but you already knew that. Everyone knows everything in Hickory Creek."

Ollie gives me an arrogant frown. "I live in Common Bend."

"And work in Hickory Creek."

"You should move to Common Bend. I could help you put down the money for a little place somewhere safe."

"I like Lush Gardens."

"What does your mother think about your new boyfriend?"

"She thinks he's hot." Though Ollie gives me an eye roll, I don't react. Instead, I add, "Mom wants me to be happy."

"That man won't marry you."

"My parents were married and ended up divorced. Marriage is overrated."

Ollie shakes his head. "He'll leave you living in a trailer park with a kid like your sisters."

153

"Camden comes from solid stock. I could do worse than to have his genetically superior kid."

"If you have a baby, you won't be able to work in downtown Nashville."

Now, I'm the one frowning. "I'm fairly sure lots of people with kids work in downtown Nashville," I say and then wipe my mouth. "Wait, are you saying if I date Camden and have his bastard, I can't work at your buddy's firm?"

"No, I'm not saying that. You're my only child, and I want you to succeed."

"You mean, as compared to Sally, who has three kids, so she doesn't care if I succeed."

"Your mother holds a different view of success."

"Your versions of success might be different, but you're both happy. I'd say that puts you on equal footing."

"I want you to be careful with this man. You know what his family does."

"Shouldn't you want me to date a rich guy? He comes from the Hallstead family, and that makes him royalty in this part of the state."

"He takes after his father."

"Physically, yes, but he's a Hallstead up here," I say, tapping my head. "You don't know him, so maybe we should stop chatting up his pros and cons."

Ollie might look like a hobo and have the breath of one, too, but he's a decent lawyer and wins a lot. Maybe this is why he thinks he can bitch his way into winning this argument with me.

"I thought Sally didn't like bikers."

"I never heard that. It could be true. I do know how she feels about lawyers."

"Funny, Daisy."

Grinning, I finish my drink. "I appreciate you getting me this job lead. I'll call him on Monday."

"You should be working somewhere better than a tanning salon."

"Don't forget it's a laundromat, too."

My dad grudgingly smiles. "You're a smart young woman. I still think you would have aced college."

"Probably, but I didn't want the debt."

"I hate thinking of you settling when you don't have to."

"How can you say I'm settling? I'm trying to get that job in downtown Nashville. Oh, and I'm dating a rich, hot man with powerful connections. If anything, I might be aiming too high in life."

Dad stands up, signaling our monthly lunch is over. "It's like talking to your mother. You're always right. You never back down. There's no reason to discuss things."

"Sorry. I didn't mean to make you sad," I say, grinning as I throw out my trash. "I forget how sensitive you can be."

My father is an old-school man. He's not tough but likes to pretend he could hold his own in a fight. It's how he was raised. No feelings, all action. Except once he bawled his eyes out, and Sally can't stop telling people the story.

"His entire face was covered with snot!" she always cries in her accented voice. "And he wanted me to hug him. I'll let children wipe snot on me but not a grown man. Can you imagine?"

I suspect every day since then, Ollie wishes he hadn't shown such weakness around a woman he planned to railroad in the divorce hearings. Though Sally got screwed with alimony and child support, she made sure everyone in Hickory Creek Township knew her ex-husband wailed like a colicky baby. Not only did everyone know, but they never let him forget it, either.

No wonder Ollie hates Hickory Creek.

TWENTY EIGHT - CAMDEN

Once again, Dayton blows me off. If I were the insecure type, his bullshit would hurt my feelings. He claims something came up, but I learn through the grapevine he's showing JJ around town. Why my brother hid this information from me is obvious. I view JJ as a threat to our claim on the club and Hickory Creek. Dayton, though, wants a new wingman to help him chase tail.

In the past, when I got pissed, I'd look for a fight or a quick fuck. They provided temporary relief to temporary problems. Now, I need the kind of soothing only Daisy's presence offers.

Waiting for her to get home from a job interview, I can't believe she still watches TV on an old CRT set. I ought to upgrade a few things at her trailer. The better plan would be to have her move into my place where everything is new. Though I don't know how Daisy would feel about moving, I figure it can't hurt to ask.

Daisy texts me to say traffic is slowing her down. Until she arrives, I watch TV on an old set with the cats surrounding me on the couch. One of the boys is curled up on my lap. I can't keep the cats' names straight. I know Seoul is the mom because I think of her being the "soul" of the family. No way could I pick her out of a cat lineup, though. They're all black and white. One has a little orange on its face, but that doesn't help me.

When I pet the cat on my lap, he purrs because cats don't give a shit about their names. Dogs are cooler, but there's something to be said for a cat's indifference.

An hour later, Daisy arrives in a rage. I hear her complaining before the door is open.

"People drive for crap," she announces.

Nudging the cat off my lap, I walk to her and kiss away the frown on her face. "Who did you wrong, Bourbon Babe?"

Her eyes lose their anger, brightening for me. "No one. I just can't stand going downtown and dealing with bad drivers. Everyone knows the lane is about to end, but there's always someone who wants to cut in line."

"Assholes. You should get their plates, so I can hunt them down and teach them a lesson."

"Funny," she says, kicking off her boots.

Daisy isn't wearing her usual fishnets and shorts. She's gone working girl with an ugly blue pants suit. I reach down and pull up the bottom of her slacks to find mismatched printed socks underneath.

"Knew it," I say.

"I couldn't find any professional-looking socks at the Goodwill."

"I'd have given you money, so you didn't need to buy this thing," I mutter, pulling at the top.

"I don't want your money, and it wouldn't matter anyhow. The interview was a bust."

"What happened?" I ask, following her into the bedroom where she strips.

"The guy who interviewed me was a butt nugget. He knew I didn't have any experience when he agreed to meet me," she grumbles, yanking free of the thick blue top. "So, I get there, and he says they're looking for someone with a four-year degree and at least two years of experience. I'm like, 'Are you frigging kidding? You want all that for a twenty-four thousand a year job?' When he acted impressed by his law firm's reputation, I just rolled my eyes. At that point, I figured I wasn't getting the job, so I didn't need to be polite anymore."

Daisy tugs free from her bulky pants and continues complaining, "I mean, who the fudge gives a fart about the firm's reputation when it comes to a translating job. I'd get it if I were a new lawyer wanting to work my way up, but I'm there to translate documents and meet with Spanish-speaking clients. Oh, and this fancy-schmancy law firm is located right next to a bail bond office. No way are they getting big

157

deal clients. I'd guess a lot of DUIs and spousal abuse cases. Doesn't matter since I was just pissed to have wasted my time."

"I'm sorry," I say, cupping her bra-covered tit. "You look sexy."

"I'm standing in my underwear and socks."

"Yeah."

"I'm sweaty."

"You'll be sweatier in a minute," I murmur, tugging down her bra straps and freeing her tits.

"Camden, I'm not in the mood."

"You always say that, and I always get you in the mood."

Daisy glares at me. "I'm crabby and want a shower. Ice cream would be nice, too."

"Afterward," I whisper, leaning down to suck at her jaw. "You're so hot when you're pissed. I need to fuck."

Daisy pulls away and gives me a darker frown. I figure she doesn't like the word "fuck" to describe us together.

"Is 'hump' better?" I ask.

Daisy's frown never falters.

"How about 'make tender love'? Do you prefer that, babe?"

I see a flicker of humor in her hazel eyes.

"Oh, I've got it," I say, popping my jeans, shoving them down, and releasing my cock from its cage. "I want our souls to touch through our crotches."

Laughing, Daisy glances down at my erect manhood. She's weighing her options. I help her decide by reaching around and undoing the hooks on her bra. After she's topless, I kick off my shoes and pants while yanking my shirt over my head.

"Seems like a waste of all this nudity if we don't become one in the nether regions."

"You need to stop talking," she says, reaching up and kissing me.

One of my hands wraps around her waist as the other yanks down her panties. Daisy can't break free from the death grip of her underwear and finally flops onto the bed to wrestle them off.

"I can help," I murmur, climbing over her. "You'd be surprised by my tongue's many uses."

I slide my body along hers, warming our skin and giving my cock a delicious taste of what's to come.

"I'm glad you were here when I got home. You make everything better."

"I know I do," I tease before covering her mouth and stealing her breath.

Daisy slides her fingers through my hair. "I'm not that mad about the job. I would rather work in a school with kids than at a law firm."

"You'll find a place."

I sense Daisy wants to tell me something. Putting my lips in neutral, I stare into her eyes. She looks back and smiles at me but says nothing.

"You'll tell me later," I promise her, and Daisy narrows her gaze at my challenge.

Before she can get too irritated, I return to kissing her. Daisy wraps her arms around my neck and gives in to my hunger. By the time I lower myself on the bed so I can explore, she's putty in my hands.

Her dark nipples shine after my tongue teases them. Even as hard points, they seem delicate to me. Everything about Daisy is fragile in my mind. She puts on a tough act, but she isn't a tough chick. I never understood the saying about someone "wearing their heart on their sleeve." I thought it meant people who freely shared, and everyone I knew was a loudmouth, but I doubted they fit the saying.

With Daisy, I understand. What she loves, she loves fiercely. Her family, cats, the crappy 1980s music, and even this trailer are hers. When she speaks of them, her gaze shines.

Now, I realize she's the same way with me. When we're together, her gaze is entirely open, even while fearing what my cock might do to her still-learning pussy. She trusts me, and I suspect she already loves me.

"Wait, stop, no, don't stop," she babbles as my cock slides inside her. "Yes."

Daisy's eyes close like they always do when she feels pleasure. I fucking love the way her face looks right now. Hell, if she'd let me, I'd grab my phone and take a picture of the blissful expression she's wearing. I'd even make the shot my screensaver. Nothing in my life makes me as proud as when Daisy comes hard, as if I healed her deep inside.

TWENTY NINE - CAMDEN

The perfect job for Daisy is available in the next town. I want her to get the position since she'll work at an excellent school in a safe neighborhood. While she already submitted her application, I can't leave her success to chance. My woman has small dreams, and I'm a failure as a man if I can't give her everything she wants.

Unfortunately, Angus Hayes is the asshole running the town over. Unlike Common Bend, which feels like the Wild West many days, and Hickory Creek, which is like Wild West's slightly better behaving cousin, White Horse is picturesque and efficient. Though all three towns are essentially controlled by dictators, Hayes does the best job of scaring the shit out of his people. I also suspect his tranquility is built on the large elderly population. Old-timers rarely riot over a traffic stop.

I drive into White Horse without giving Hayes a heads-up. He likes knowing when the club guys are in his territory. But I'm not his fucking bitch, and he ought to learn how to deal with surprises better.

His office is a bunker-style monstrosity that fits the man to a T. I admire anyone so willing to forgo style to make himself harder to kill.

Inside, I find his assistant and new wife. Candy is another reason I don't call ahead. The blonde refuses to take messages and often calls me by women's names, even though she knows exactly who the fuck I am.

"He's dead," she says, prying her eyes away from a game of PC solitaire to look at me. "We were all shocked and ask for our privacy at this difficult time. Thanks for understanding. Now, get out."

"He's a bad influence on you," I say, crossing my arms.

"He wishes," Candy mutters. "What do you want?"

"I need to talk to your old man."

"He's dead, so that'll be tricky. Know any psychics?"

161

"I hear him in the back office."

Candy never misses a beat. "That's his ghost. You didn't think he'd go quietly, did you?"

"Be a good little girl and scoot your ass to the back and tell him I need to talk to him. If he doesn't talk to me today, I'll keep coming back. That'll be more work for you, so I guess you ought to be scooting."

"Sure, Dayton."

"Funny."

"Wait, which one are you, then?"

"Just get Hayes."

Candy grins at my irritation and then leans back in her chair. "You have a visitor!"

"I see that!" Hayes hollers back.

"I'd kick his ass, but anyone over six feet is above my pay grade."

"I'm not giving you a raise!"

"Stop flirting with each other!" I yell and begin toward the back office. "It's not nearly as cute to other people."

Huge and imposing, Hayes sits behind his desk and puffs on a cigar. His step-kids stand at the window. The boy and girl twins turn in unison and stare at me.

"Save the creepy twin shit," I mutter. "I did that crap when I was a kid, and it's not nearly as effective if you don't match."

The dark-haired girl frowns. "Your sister is identical to you?"

Rolling my eyes, I sit across from Hayes. "Can you make them leave?"

"I can do whatever I want, turd, but I'm their teacher, and this is a good lesson for them," he says and looks at the twins. "Today's lesson deals with disappointment. Let's see if Rutgers handles it without crying."

"I have a favor to ask."

"No."

"A personal favor. Don't you want to teach the creepy kids the benefit of having powerful people owe you?"

Hayes puffs at his cigar and considers my words. He gestures for me to continue.

"I have a woman, and she needs a job."

"I don't own any strip clubs."

"Funny and a lie." Glancing at the twins, I add, "He's lying, you know?"

"Yeah, but we don't care," says the blond boy.

"Are you sure they're not your bio kids?" I ask Hayes, who frowns.

"Make your pitch, Rutgers."

"The Berrywood Elementary School is looking for someone to work with the Spanish-speaking kids. My woman is fluent in Spanish. She needs a job, and I want her to work somewhere safe. Your town offers me that, so I'm giving you the opportunity to have me owe you."

"Why can't she get the job on her own?"

"She lacks experience. Her resume is full of doctor's offices and laundromats. She's the real deal with translating, though. She'll work hard, and you won't need to bail her out for mistakes or any of that shit. Just get her in the door, and she'll do the job right."

"And you'll owe me a favor. That'd be more appealing if you were the big dick in Hickory Creek."

Leaning back in the chair, I hold his gaze. "I will be soon enough. When I am, I'll have my eye on southern territory rather than going north to Common Bend and White Horse. So, I'm not only a good person to have owe you, but I'm a potential ally for your heirs here."

The twins look at their step-dad and then back at me. They're unimpressed, but Hayes seems ready to give Daisy the job. A small move on his part could come back to help him big time later. He didn't get ahead by passing up easy opportunities.

"What if your brother becomes president?"

"The only way that happens is if I'm dead, and I plan to live a long fucking time."

"Other people might plan something different for you, boy."

"No doubt, they do. Planning something and making it happen are two very different fucking things."

Hayes isn't done messing with my head, even if he's ready to agree to my deal. "Your old man and uncle still have their greedy eyes on Common Bend. I don't want their bullshit spreading."

"Neither do I. Taking Common Bend means going to war with another club. That's a lot of collateral damage for little payoff. I don't have to be ancient like you to know that much."

Hayes grins. "Balls are a wonderful thing, but you better be careful not to write checks your testicles can't cash. You have Mojo, Howler, and your idiot brother standing in your way to claim the crown."

"You let me worry about that. You just concern yourself with getting my woman the job."

Hayes stands up and puts out his cigar. "Even if your dad is around or your brother becomes president, I can see how an olive branch to you could be helpful to me. I'll get your woman her job, but I won't clean up anything for her. She does the work, or she's out. I'm no one's babysitter."

"Good," I say and extend my hand to shake his. "The future is nearly present, and I think we have the potential for a solid relationship. Until then, let's keep our flirting private. I don't need anything causing my club to cannibalize itself."

"What does 'cannibalize' mean?" the boy asks.

"Google it," Hayes says and walks me out of the room. "Next time you want to chat, call first. I'll make sure Candy puts the call through. That's just you. Not your daddy or brother and certainly not your horndog uncle. I can be cooperative, but not that fucking cooperative."

Walking to the door while he stands next to Candy, I glance back. "It's always a pleasure, Mister and Missus Hayes."

"He has pretty hair," Candy says as I exit.

164

"Next time, you can ask him for beauty tips," Hayes replies.

Leaving them to their flirting, I wear a big fucking smile while riding Shasta back to Hickory Creek. Daisy needed something, and I got it for her. I can think of nothing more invigorating than providing for my woman.

THIRTY - DAISY

Mylie Anders was one of the popular girls in high school. While she had no interest in me, she always kissed Ruby's ass. Oh, and she hated Harmony. Most girls in high school loathed my younger sister. She was too naturally beautiful and easygoing. While the teenage years were horrible for most people, Harmony floated through her awkward phase without much trouble. Yeah, I'd probably have hated her a little, too, if I didn't love her so much.

I don't know why Mylie invites us to her bachelorette blowout in Common Bend. She seems especially keen on Ruby attending. My older sister had a cool vibe in high school. She didn't care what anyone thought, giving her power the popular girls couldn't claim. Ruby was also dating Bonn, who never suffered an awkward moment in his life. He was born gorgeous, and no doubt, looked sexy while taking a crap. Those Hallstead men were easily flawless like Harmony.

Mylie begged and nagged until Ruby agreed to attend the party. Not wanting to be stuck for hours with only women she didn't like, she asked Harmony and me to suffer with her.

I've never been to a bachelorette party. I expect something smaller with a dozen women drinking while the bride opens gifts. Instead, Mylie's friends throw her a massive party to celebrate her upcoming marriage to a real medical doctor. I swear I hear three times in the first ten minutes his profession but never his name.

We arrive at the two-story house to the booming beat of Coolio's "Gangsta's Paradise." Harmony whispers to me something about white girls wanting to play tough bitches. I nod at her comment and take a cup filled with spiked punch.

"We give it an hour," Ruby says, "and then bail."

"Aren't you having fun?" Harmony asks, shaking her butt to the beat and bumping our grumpier older sister. "If

166

you fake like you're happy, she'll throw less of a tantrum when you want to leave."

"I don't know why Mylie even cares if I'm here. We were barely friends in high school, and that was years ago."

"Who knows?" I say. "Old people confuse me."

Ruby dips her fingers in her drink and flicks them at me. I try to duck away from the sticky drops, but I'm too slow, and my feet are too big. I nearly fall on my ass, trying to avoid getting a tiny bit wet. Ruby and Harmony laugh at me. Even embarrassed by my lack of skill, I still take a bow.

"It all comes naturally," I say.

Ruby loses her smile. "Bitch at four o'clock."

"I don't know what four o'clock means," I mutter, glancing around.

"I think it means behind you," Harmony says, being unhelpful since I look behind me and find a wall.

"I see no bitch. Is she invisible? Do you think I'm Superman and can see through walls?"

Harmony laughs while Ruby narrows her eyes and glares in the direction of the bitch. I finally locate four o'clock when I spot Brittany Sams.

The rumor-spreading blonde butt-stain sees me seeing her, and she smiles like a fucking crazy person mocking the victim in her car trunk. I smile back at her like I assume Camden looked at Lincoln before busting his head open.

"I'm going to say hello."

"Why?" Ruby grumbles.

"Whatever do you mean? I'm a warm, outgoing person who loves my fellow American women people. Now, fuck off while I go chat up the butt-stain."

My sisters laugh at my comment, but Ruby still makes one last-ditch effort to grab me. I dodge her hand, nearly falling on my face before eventually reaching Brittany. I stare into the eyes of the bitch-stain whose lie traumatized me into eating salad for frigging months. I can't be sure I won't kill her. I mean, I'm fairly sure I won't, but I did eat a lot of damn salad.

"I was hoping we'd run into each other," I say. "Everything going okay with you?"

The blonde shit-stain grins, and I notice a little lipstick on her teeth. "Yeah, I'm great."

"Has anyone been treating you weird?"

Her smile fades, and her blue eyes narrow. "Why?"

"No reason. I just figured people might be looking at you in a weird way. Or treating you differently. I'm happy to hear you haven't noticed anything yet. I don't want Mylie's party to get awkward."

"What the fuck are you talking about?" she demands, and I worry she'll splash her drink at me.

"Since I'm dating Camden, I'm not holding a grudge anymore."

"I don't know what you heard, but—"

Leaning closer, I growl, "Are you calling Camden a liar because I will so snitch you out for talking shit about him?"

Brittany repeatedly opens her mouth to respond but changes her mind each time. Finally, she exhales really hard, and I'm hit in the face by a smell that makes me think of Camden or maybe the back of the school bleachers.

"Why does your breath smell like semen?" I balk, stepping back. "No, don't answer that."

"Shut the fuck up."

"Did I hurt your feeling? If your answer is no, well, give it time, cum-breath."

"I didn't even start the rumor because of you. I did it because of Harmony. She's a stupid whore who stole my boyfriend."

"How does starting a rumor about me being fat hurt my skinny sister, who your high school boyfriend wanted more than you?"

Brittany again thinks about responding, but she's flustered from too much liquor and too little knowledge about how bad at fighting I am. If she had any idea how easily I'd fall over if she poked me, I bet I'd already be on my ass.

168

Storming away from me, Brittany leaves an odd smell in her place. I hurry back to my sisters and frown at them.

"Do I smell like semen after I've been with Camden?"

Ruby smirks. "Daisy, I don't go around sniffing people."

"I do," Harmony says, clearly having downed her drink and smiling way too much, "And you smell like happiness after you've been with Camden."

Ruby and I burst into laughter. I laugh so hard I think I might pee. It'd be less funny if Harmony weren't serious. Booze turns her into a dippy hippy.

For the next ten minutes, I have the best time with my sisters. We drink the spiked punch and reenact my smack talk with Brittany. My threats get cooler with each retelling.

Before we have too much fun, Mylie appears with her bridesmaids. They're wearing crowns, glitter, and matching "DIVA" T-shirts. I let myself imagine getting married to Camden and wonder if I'd be as obnoxious as these twats. Deciding I would, I nearly miss Mylie's announcement about the strippers arriving.

Helpfully, she yells, "The man-meat is here to shake their asses and long dong silvers!"

"I haven't seen a long dong silver in a long, damn time," Harmony whispers to me.

"You're lying."

"A little, but I'm still horny."

Laughing at my buzzed sister, I keep her at arm's length so she doesn't use my leg for her jollies. Ruby watches us both, and I know she's annoyed. If anyone deserves pity for going too long without a dick near their vaginal area, Ruby should get the telethon.

I'm busy teasing my sisters in the corner of the living room when the strippers arrive with their signature "Let's Get It Started" song. I start laughing at the thought of swinging dong, and Harmony nearly falls on her ass giggling next to me. Ruby is also having a good time until suddenly she isn't. Instantly, she looks ready to shift into a giant, green monster and tear up the damn place.

"What?" I ask, using the wall to keep me upright. "Who turned you into the Hulk?"

Ruby's smoky brown eyes stare at me as she shakes her head. When she opens her mouth to speak, only a squeaky noise comes out. I look around, wondering whose ass I need to kick.

Bonn Fletcher makes a fetching cop, even if his uniform has tear-away pants. I suddenly understand how he's able to live in the same condo complex as Camden. Bonn has the body to be a stripper, but that doesn't make the shock any easier for Ruby. Even after all these years, she remains hung up on her first love.

"I need to get out of here," she says when I wrap an arm around her shoulders.

Nodding, I set down my drink, grab Harmony, and start making our way through the crowd of chanting women. I hear someone calling Ruby's name, but we never stop moving. Harmony grips my shirt to keep from losing us in the crowded room. We're nearly at the door when Ruby can't ignore Mylie's voice any longer.

I turn to find the party paused so everyone can look at the bride chasing us. Ruby doesn't even see Mylie. Her gaze is locked on Bonn's. The former lovers share a mental conversation. Bonn doesn't flinch or show a hint of fear at having his big secret outed. Ruby can't hide her feelings nearly as well.

"Don't you want to see your baby daddy dance for us?" Mylie asks, barely containing her evil glee.

Ruby stares at Bonn, completely oblivious to Mylie. I feel like I should say or do something. Normally, I'd let Harmony play peacemaker, but my younger sis looks ready to puke. Besides, half the bitches at the party hold a grudge against her.

"For fucks sake!" I holler. "High school ended a long time ago, ladies!"

I grab Ruby's hand and snag one of Harmony's before pulling them out the front door. People follow us, and I don't know if we'll get to the car before Ruby loses her shit. My older sister's reaction can go two ways—brokenhearted tears or swinging-for-the-bitches-rage.

"Ruby, wait," Bonn says, hurrying to stop us. "I didn't know you'd be here."

"Would it have mattered?" Ruby demands, finding her voice and apparently leaning toward a rage reaction.

"I only work outside of Hickory Creek. I never wanted you or Chevelle to know," he says and then adds, "I needed the money."

"What about your dad? Think he'll be okay with your side job?"

Bonn's expression flickers, revealing genuine fear. Recovering his emotionless expression, he shrugs his big shoulders. "You do what you want."

"I will as always, asshole."

Ruby storms away as Harmony and I run to catch up.

"A stripper," she mutters, fumbling with her car keys.

I take them from her and pull Ruby into a hug. "I'm sorry."

"It's fine. He's not mine. What do I care what he does?"

"Are you going to tell his dad?"

Fighting tears, Ruby shakes her head. "His dad treats him like shit. I'm not giving Howler any ammo to make it worse."

As much as I want to comfort Ruby, the damn party remains focused on us. Mainly because Mylie is still enjoying her ridiculous revenge against Ruby for some long-ago offense.

Harmony stumbles into the back seat. "The bitch is coming."

Ruby shakes her head and walks around to the driver's side. Rather than get into the car, I face a glowing Mylie.

"That was a bitch move," I say.

"I didn't realize Ruby would be upset. I figured seeing him shake his ass would bring back good memories."

Her friends snicker at her comment, but I'm uninterested in them. I'm too busy thinking about how much bullshit from high school still taints our lives. Everyone remains mad about some stupid thing or another. Even this grown woman on the verge of marrying above her pay grade can't avoid taking a swipe at a girl who pissed her off nearly ten years earlier.

"You should be more careful about how you treat people, Mylie. Especially when you have such an important day coming. It'd be a real shame for something bad to happen at your wedding."

"Are you threatening me?"

"I'm just saying a lot of things can go wrong at a wedding. The food, an unexpected guest, your dress, a no-show groom. So many things."

Stepping closer, Mylie loses her smile. "You best not be threatening me."

"Or you'll what?" I say, erasing the space between us. "Will you sic your bridesmaids on me? I suggest you focus your energy on the big day."

Mylie points her finger at me and growls, "I'm warning you."

"I'm warning you right back, bitch!" I holler, losing my temper and feeling damn good about it. "You better stop wagging your fat fingers in my face and bugging your ugly eyes at me, or I'll rip off those cheap-ass nails and use them to clean out your eye sockets."

Mylie freezes, and I feel her friends go quiet, too. Camden told me once how overly specific threats freak out people. You claim you'll beat the shit out of a guy, and he'll shrug you off. You claim you'll shove your stinky sock down a guy's throat, and he'll wonder why you'd be so specific unless you meant it.

I get the same reaction from Mylie and her friends, which is a good thing since I'm terrified she'll use those cheap-ass nails to claw out my eyes. If she hits me, my sisters will jump into the fight. Then, the bridesmaids will join the battle. I'll end up a bloody ball on the floor watching my sisters battle sloppy-drunk chicks. Since I'm not a fan of that scenario, I stand firm while Mylie backs down.

"You should enjoy your party," I tell Mylie. "Stop all this fussing and feuding and hope for the best outcome you can still get."

The bitch flips me off and storms away, but I know she'll spend her entire wedding day waiting for my payback. I don't know if such revenge will be enough for Ruby. Hell, Mylie might even need to worry about Bonn's temper.

For now, I focus on Ruby. Once I get into the car, she hits the gas and speeds away from the house and out of Common Bend.

"I think that drink was spiked with more than booze," Harmony says, leaning over in the car.

"Do you need to puke?" I ask.

"No, but I feel weird."

I reach back to rub Harmony's head, but my gaze is on Ruby. Seeing her hands wrapped in a death grip around the steering wheel, I don't know if I should push her to talk or let her stew in her thoughts.

"I don't know why I care," she says once we're home with Harmony tucked in bed.

I stand next to my sister and wish I had a clue what to tell her.

"You care because you loved him."

"I keep waiting to get over him."

"Bonn is special, but he fucked up."

Nodding, Ruby leaves Harmony to sleep off the twice-spiked punch. "How do you feel? You drank that punch, too."

"I only had one cup. I'm buzzed but not overly so. Maybe they only drugged Harmony."

"They're so stupid," Ruby says, sitting on the couch with her knees pressed against her chest. "Harmony has a kid now. She has a job taking care of sick, old people. She's got a damn grown-up life, and those bitches are still mad their high school boyfriends all wanted to nail her."

"What was Mylie's deal with you?"

"She's always been really into getting my approval. Probably because I was the one person who didn't care about her crap. When she invited me to the party, I guess I didn't make a big enough deal of it. She likes to show off, but I'm not impressed. Why do I care what other people have or don't have? I only care about my life, no one else's."

I know Ruby is thinking about Bonn and how she still cares about his life.

"I don't think construction pays much during the off-season."

"No," Ruby says, wrapping her arms around her legs. "He wants to live up to a stupid idea in his head. As if Chevelle would love him any less if he lived in a smaller place or drove an older car. She doesn't care about any of that. You know how much she adores him."

"His dad fucked up his thinking."

"Yeah, and his mom always focused on what they didn't have. How they lived in a tiny apartment while Jude lived in a giant house. She was bitter, and he got it into his head how he has something to prove."

"It's easy money, and he did take those dance classes growing up."

Ruby struggles against a smile. I laugh at the thought of Bonn taking ballet classes as a kid and now shaking his ass for drunken women. Ruby finally gives in and giggles, too.

"His mom forced him to take those dance classes as a way to piss off Jude. I don't think she thought he'd use the lessons this way."

"Think she knows?"

"No way."

"Can't imagine he thought his secret would stay secret long. People talk, and there can't be that many male strippers, and he's damn hot. No offense."

174

"Why would I be offended by his hotness?"

"I didn't want to rub it in your face."

"Like he's rubbing his junk in Mylie's face?"

Though I really, really don't want to laugh, the image she paints sends me into hysterics.

"Oh, poor, hot, Bonn," I mumble, laughing.

"The bitch better tip him well."

"Once his pants come off, I'm sure they'll all tip him well. I'd probably shove a twenty in his panties if we'd stuck around."

Ruby laughs. "It is easy money. If it helps him out, I should be happy for him."

"You aren't, though."

"No fucking way. He broke my heart. I want his life to suck, but not so much that it affects Chevelle," she says and then sighs. "I'm a fucking idiot."

"Sure, but you're in good company. We're all fucking idiots. I was threatening people left and right tonight, and I can't fight for shit. Harmony is a fucking idiot because she's effortlessly attractive, and that's not fair to the rest of us. Bonn is a fucking idiot for losing you. Mylie is a fucking idiot because she exists."

Ruby pats my hand. "I have to say Camden's been a bad influence on you, and I really like the results."

"Thanks. He gives me confidence."

"Aren't you supposed to find that from within?"

"I don't know."

"Me either, but that's what I tell Chevelle. She is the only one who can bring her happiness or some shit. Fifty percent of parenthood is lying, so children don't turn jaded before hitting their teenage years."

"Sounds easy."

"Shut up," she says, flicking my nose. "Shut the fuck up so hard."

"Are you feeling jealous that my man is totally into me, and you're alone lying to your kid?"

Ruby hits me in the face with a throw pillow. I try to duck the second strike and fall off the couch. Laughing, she tackles me and pins my arms to the floor.

"You're so weak," she teases.

"I ate a lot of salad these last few months."

"That'll do it."

"I'm sorry about tonight."

Ruby nods. "I like that you stood up for me."

"I was pretty awesome."

"Can you imagine if someone called your bluff?"

"I'd get my ass kicked, and then I'd whine to Camden. I wonder what he'd do."

Ruby slides off me and smiles. "Maybe you should find out."

Sitting up, I consider siccing my criminal boyfriend on the stupid bitch. "What would you want to happen to Mylie?"

"I meant Brittany."

"Oh, I won that. She's a lonely, bitter poop-stain who smells like semen. I'm dating a hot guy and have great sisters and a fun mom and three cats who worship me as their maid."

"You truly are living the dream."

"Should I ask Camden to do something to Mylie?" I whisper, feeling evil for even suggesting it.

Ruby shrugs. "Probably not. Mom says it's bad to owe rich people things."

"Mom also claims her dog cries when she does."

Laughing, Ruby falls back on the floor. She giggles wildly until the night's tensions wash away. I hang out with her for another hour, watching TV and eating popcorn. We take turns checking on Harmony, who never stirs.

The night feels overwhelming yet anticlimactic. Walking to my trailer, I miss Camden and wish he was sleeping over tonight. I even think to text him to come over. I feel guilty for expecting him to drop everything for me and decide to shower rather than making the call.

Midnight arrives with me watching "House Hunters International." I've replayed the night's events a million times. I imagine saying different things. I also picture getting my ass kicked. In the end, I can only think of Ruby and Bonn.

If Camden dumps me, I'll end up no different than my sister. I'll never recover. I'll never date another guy. *What would be the point?* I'd compare any man to Camden. No one would live up to him.

He's ruined me, and I'm okay with that. Life doesn't always end with rainbows and flowers. Sometimes, an amazing journey is enough. I know without a doubt how Ruby wouldn't change her time with Bonn, even knowing how things ended. All her pain was worth it. Whatever happens between Camden and me, I will never regret every moment we've spent together.

THIRTY ONE - CAMDEN

I promise Daisy I'll give her another night of freedom. She claims I'm clingy. I call my behavior good old-fashioned possessiveness. She says I want to keep my secrets, so I need to allow her a few of her own. I don't agree with her, but she pulls off her shirt and wins another argument. This new tactic of hers is killing me, and I need to get the hang of seeing her perky tits without losing my brain.

So, while she spends Saturday at a bachelorette party with her sisters, I need to keep myself busy. A few weeks ago, I was capable of being alone at night. Now, I'm restless like a cranky baby. Eating out alone, I watch a fussy kid at the next table and feel his pain. *Why is it so difficult for people to just give us what we want?*

Later, I spot Dayton at Salty Peanuts, but he gives me a dark glare when I make a move to join him and his lady friend. He's also restless lately, but not because he has a woman on the brain. Or maybe he does.

Dayton and I are currently on the outs. He thinks I've lost my mind by wanting Daisy. I think he's lost his for thinking we can spend a life single like Dad. I doubt he wants to be alone forever, but his worship of our father knows no bounds.

After Salty Peanuts, I make my way around town, checking various businesses and looking for anyone in the mood to stir up shit. For years, Hickory Creek hummed along without any sign of trouble. Then, Common Bend lost their sheriff and gained a new rogue one. Suddenly, the nearby town was in play. Mojo and Howler regained their hard-ons for taking over Common Bend. When that didn't happen, they remained on edge. They want something, but I suspect nothing will satisfy except the little shithole next door.

With the club's top guys radiating unease, the rest of Hickory Creek feeds on it and reacts in small ways. The pimp slaps his girls in public. The dealer skims a little more off the top before handing over profits to the Brotherhood. Businesses get slower about paying protection funds. Mom says people never stop being children. When kids sense weakness in their parents, they test boundaries.

I notice this boundary-testing when I show up at one business after another. The owners are slow to acknowledge me. They claim they're busy and ask me to return another time. I know such bullshit didn't fly in my father's heyday, and it won't fly with me.

"Are you hoping I'll bend over so you can fuck me?" I ask the owner of Barry's Spaghetti House. "I only ask because you're looking at me like your bitch."

Barry's bored expression shifts into one of pure terror. He's like a kid after Mom and Dad yank off the belt. Yeah, I'm not playing, and the Brotherhood isn't going soft. Not while I'm one of the soldiers and certainly not when I become president.

Tonight, I make a lot of bitchy kids shit their pants. Working distracts me from thoughts of Daisy for only so long. I need to know where she is right at that moment. Who is she talking to? Are men at the party? Is anyone flirting with her? Who do I need to kill?

By eleven, I've threatened enough business owners to make them at least fear me. Maybe they still think my old man is a big softie. They're reading him wrong, of course, but I'm not his PR person. He can scare them himself.

I end up back at Salty Peanuts because I don't know where else to go. Bonn is working tonight. Dayton is acting like a douche. I think to hang out with Mom. Except she spends Saturdays watching chick films, and I can't sit through "Fried Green Tomatoes" again.

When I notice JJ enter the bar, I play blind. He's my least favorite person these days. I spot his guys hanging around every place I visit tonight. Apparently, JJ ran a crew out of Birmingham. When he came to meet his long-lost daddy, he decided to bring all his buddies. This setup reeks of bullshit to me, but avoiding JJ is my current game plan. Unfortunately, avoiding me doesn't occur to JJ.

"Hello, cousin," he says with a level of familiarity I'm uncomfortable with.

I don't know this guy, and nothing about his demeanor makes me want to. He's a slimy common thug. I bet at least some of his early work involved stealing old ladies' social security checks. JJ isn't my kind of guy, and nothing is bound to change my mind about him.

"How is Hickory Creek treating you?" I ask in a voice devoid of interest.

"Very well, indeed. I can see why Dad loves it here so much."

His overly familiar vibe with Howler feels all wrong. What kind of tough guy melts over a man who fucked and abandoned his mom? Howler never did shit for Bonn, who lived in Hickory Creek. No way did he do shit for JJ. Just because this fucker's mom was stupid enough to name him Jude Junior doesn't make him Howler's favorite. Yet, somehow this dumbass runs around town acting as the heir-apparent.

"Good to hear," I say rather than throttling the asshole.

"I'm planning to stick around. I'm sure that's obvious, but I wanted to make it clear just in case you weren't in the loop."

In the loop? This guy is begging for a broken face.

"No offense, man, but you hanging around isn't newsworthy. Howler has a bunch of kids, and they show up occasionally. I'm all for you bonding with your dad, but I have a business to run."

JJ never loses his smile, and I realize this guy is a stone-cold killer. No way does he look in my irritated eyes without flinching unless he figures he's capable of taking me down.

"Speaking of business, Dad is talking about having me patched into the club."

"Based on what?" I ask, ordering a drink and stomping down my temper. Since JJ wants to be chatty, I sense I better listen up. "Guys get patched in for the work they do for the club. You haven't done any yet."

"Oh, I know about loyalty."

"Then, why is your old crew around?" I ask, glancing at one of the fuckers sitting at a table in the back. "If you want to join the Brotherhood, you need to cut ties to any group that could divide your loyalty. Then you need to break a sweat for the club and prove yourself worthy. I didn't get patched in because of my daddy. I had to work like everyone else. Grunt shit at the start. No one gets patched into the Brotherhood based on a DNA test. That's just not how it's done."

"Fair enough," JJ says, giving off a dangerously friendly vibe.

"You have experience with busting balls, I'm sure. So, you ought to have no problem embracing grunt work. Cut loose your old ties, settle in here, and shit ought to work out fine."

JJ nods at the false friendship bullshit I'm selling. He thinks I'm threatened by him, and he's right. The guy shows up and wants things handed to him. Things I had to hustle to earn. He sees me as a threat, and I view him in the same fucking way. I just wonder which one of us will pull the trigger first.

"Thanks for the advice, Dayton," he says, patting my shoulder. "I'm gonna see if I can find something pretty to warm my bed tonight."

"You do that," I reply as if he didn't use the wrong name.

I want to believe he purposely fudged the names to put me in my place, but I think he really can't tell Dayton and me apart. Most people can't.

Daisy isn't most people. She knows me and willfully ignores the parts that don't fit what she needs. That's how a club old lady needs to be. Asking questions leads to unhappy answers. Daisy doesn't care about the club. She only wants me, and I want to hook up with her tonight.

Keeping my promise, I look at my phone but never call her. I leave the bar and head to my place. Finding the condo too quiet, I wish I had a pet. Except I'm never around enough to enjoy one. Fuck pets. I'm craving one thing, and only that one thing will do. I bet she's home from her party by now.

I want nothing more than to knock on Daisy's door, wrap her in my arms, and have us spend the night naked together. JJ pisses me off, and I feel the town changing. Daisy makes that bullshit fade away. I don't know how she does it, but that's what I need right now.

Since I'm a man of my word, I don't show up at her door. I do end up driving over to the trailer park with my SUV. Parking, I crawl into the back seat, play tunes on my phone, and doze as close to my woman as I can manage without breaking my promise.

THIRTY TWO - DAISY

I take forever to fall asleep. My mind reels with the image of Bonn in his cop stripper outfit. I keep seeing Ruby's horrified expression. I also freak about how I faced down two bitches as if I could do much more than fall on my ass if they took a swing at me. Mostly, I miss Camden and wonder where he's at and if he's thinking about me.

Just after dawn, I hear a knock at the door and force my exhausted ass up. I stumble over a freaked Tokyo, who shares my horror at such an early wake-up call. Peering through the window, I discover a sleepy Camden on my porch. I throw open the door and stare in surprise.

"I kept my promise," he mumbles, entering the trailer and shutting the door. "Now, it's morning."

Wrapping my arms around his waist, I hug him with relief. "I missed you so much."

Camden smiles, seeming surprised by my reaction. "Of course, you did," he says and cups my face.

"Two nights without you is too damn much."

Kissing me, Camden nods at my statement. His lips are possessive, but I sense he's tired. As soon as our tongues disengage, I pull away and take his hand.

"A quickie, and then we nap, yes?"

"Fucking-A, yes."

Smiling, I nearly trip over Seoul. "The cats do not respond well to early mornings."

"I know how they feel."

Once in my room, we race to see who gets naked first. Considering I'm only wearing a nightgown, I win before crawling onto the bed.

"How was the party?" he asks, smiling at my butt facing him.

I flop on the bed and stretch out. "Crap. I hate everyone except my family and you."

"Sounds about right," he says, crawling over me. "People piss me off."

"Not me, right? Never me."

"Oh, never you," he teases and then covers my mouth with his.

Even sleepy, Camden consumes me. He nips and licks my naked flesh until I'm soaking wet. He knows I can't survive his size unless all my engines are firing. Once I'm running hot, he slides into me, filling my body until I wonder how I will ever walk again. The fullness sends me over the edge, and I make a noise that sends the cats running.

Camden doesn't laugh at their reaction or my impassioned cry. He's a man possessed, and I understand how our time apart hurt him too. We functioned alone for a long time, but those days are over. Now, we need each other to be happy. No more days apart or forcing promises on a man only desperate for my touch.

Thrusting wildly, Camden takes his frustration out on my jubilant pussy. I wrap my legs around his muscular hips, grab hold of the headboard, and try to survive this passionate man.

"Don't look at other men," he grunts after coming hard enough for me to worry about his health. "No other man."

"Okay," I murmur, catching my breath even if his request is silly. "All other men make me sick. I only want to look at you."

Camden smiles and rolls off. As quickly as our bodies part, he presses himself against me again. A sweaty and relaxed Camden yanks a sheet over us and smiles again.

"I slept in my SUV out in the trailer park's lot. Just thought I'd tell you since your neighbors probably spotted me. Nothing's private at Lush Gardens."

"You should have knocked earlier," I whisper, caressing his stubbled cheek. "I couldn't sleep well without you."

"I'm your man."

"Fucking-A, you are."

Camden's smile widens, but we're both tired. A nap offers relief from the fatigue. It also recharges my man, who rides me hard when we awake hours later. I ride him once too, but damn, if I'm not a lazy lover. I'd rather just stick my ass in the air and let him fuck me doggy-style while I do nothing more than hold on for dear life. Oh, and orgasm. I do that a lot, too.

After a quick breakfast, since my fridge is nearly empty, we sit on the couch and watch each other. I have things I want to tell him but fear saying them out loud. Camden might want to tell me things, too. Or he might just want to stare at me. His peaceful expression is unreadable.

"Why was the party so shitty?" he asks when I say nothing for too long.

I rush through the details about Bonn, Mylie, and Brittany. His peaceful expression shifts a few times. Anger, confusion, shock, and back to anger before he finally just grunts, "Well, fuck."

The Bonn info likely freaks him out since he has a rather idealized view of his cousin. Watching Camden process everything, I realize I love him so much I'd endure nearly anything to be his woman forever.

"Even if you lost your money and ended up working at Burger King, I'd want you," I blurt out. "And even if you had to cut off your hair and lost all your sexy muscles and ended up with a gut and acnes, I'd want you. If you went to prison, I'd wait for you."

I pause a moment, afraid to continue, but his appearance at my door this morning gives me courage.

"The way I feel about you isn't about your money or power or how fucking hot you are. If it was, I could exchange you for Dayton. There's something about you specifically that makes me feel like no one else can. It's like all the best feelings I have with my family but also with these extra needs. I'm not saying it right, I guess. I just know I love you because you make me a better person while also making me feel like I don't have to be better. Like I'm okay being me, and that's a liberating way to feel."

"If another man touches you, I'm cutting off his hands."

"I'm okay with that. What if I touch another man?"

"I'll still cut off his hands."

"What about my hands?"

Camden takes my hands in his and kisses each one. "Keep your hands off other guys, Daisy Bourbon Crest."

"I'll try, but I'm a slut, so no promises."

Even smiling, Camden has no sense of humor about other guys and me.

"No one has ever made me wet except you," I say, kissing his hands. "I could barely deal with hugging other guys, but with you, hugging will never be enough. I'm only a slut for you."

"Fucking-A, you are. I saw you wiggling that ass for me this morning."

Smiling, I think about his response to my saying I love him. I lose my smile and lift an eyebrow.

"Well?" I ask when he only stares at me.

"Let's get married."

"Why?"

"Because I want to knock you up."

"You're weird," I say, standing.

Camden takes me by the wrist and tugs me across his lap. I frown at him, but he only smiles.

"I loved you before you loved me," he says casually. "If anyone gets an award for loving, it's me. I'm the champion of love. Am I still weird?"

"More so than ever," I say, smiling.

"Let's get married."

I open my mouth to be rational, and he does the key thing. Rolling my eyes, I close my mouth and consider yanking off my shirt.

"Don't think. Just feel, Bourbon Babe. In your heart, you know we match up perfectly. We are meant to be, and no amount of shit rumors or misunderstandings can stop how we feel. Why wait so that you can feel rational? Rational is fucking overrated. We should just be. Just do what we want. Don't wait for others to give approval or for things to make sense. They already make sense in our hearts. Our brains are just filled with society's bullshit."

"That's eloquent, but—"

"But what?"

Glancing around, I struggle to steady my wildly beating heart. *Can I marry Camden Rutgers? Is that a choice I can just make on a Sunday morning without speaking to my sisters first?*

"Where would we live?"

"Who cares?"

"What if I don't want kids right away?"

"We'll argue about that later, and I'll win even if you take off your shirt."

"You'll try," I say, glancing down at my secret weapons.

Camden lifts my chin and forces me to look at him. "I'm thinking with my heart right now. Let's keep my dick out of the conversation."

"I love you."

"Then, marry me right fucking now."

"What if I want to plan a wedding?"

"You don't. You hate having everyone looking at you. You'd pull your hair out trying to pick a dress, cake, and the rest. You don't like that shit, but you think you should like that shit. That's why you'd pretend. Let's skip the pretending and just do what we want."

Crawling off his lap, I grab the imaginary key and turn my brain back on. Camden sighs, thinking he'll lose now.

"Eloping is pretty damn romantic," I say, stroking his head. "You're a romantic guy, and I'm a romantic girl. Let's do it."

Camden gives me a cocky grin. He likes winning. A little part of me worries he sees me as a prize, and he'll lose interest once he's claimed me. I should trust him, but in a million ways, we're strangers about to marry.

My mom is an impulsive woman who married her first husband on a lark during a Jamaican holiday. Life with Daniel Bauer didn't last long but did give her a daughter. Sally always says she's never regretted any of her choices.

About to take a leap of faith, I can only hope I feel the same way when I'm her age.

THIRTY THREE - DAISY

On the morning I elope with Camden, keeping my mouth shut nearly kills me. For our last night as single people, we sleep apart. This way our wedding night will be more exciting. This idea was likely mine, proving I'm an idiot with poor planning skills.

We miss each other so much we end up on the phone most of the evening. I watch "House Hunters International" episodes while Camden watches sports. I consider asking him to come over a few times. Eventually, the night gets late enough for us to crash with tomorrow on the brain.

The next morning, I keep running into my sisters as they prepare to leave for work. I want to tell them so badly about my plans. I stare at them, hoping they'll read my mind so I won't need to say the words.

Ruby teases me about my odd behavior, wondering if all the sex has injured me. Harmony pats me on the head when I struggle to speak. Despite the overpowering urge to tell them, I know if they knew, they'd want to come along. Then, Sally would join us. Next, Betty. Charlie, and Billy would show up. Soon, Camden would want his family there. Finally, our simple ceremony becomes a big frigging event.

So, I keep my big mouth shut even when Sally corners me before she goes to work.

"When do you start your new job?"

"In a few weeks. They're running a background check, but that's just a formality."

"Do you need work clothes?"

"They said khaki pants were okay. Nothing fancy."

Sally strokes a lock of my hair. "I'm glad you didn't get the job your father lined up. Owing him is never a good idea."

"I don't care about owing people. Unlike you, I lack the honor necessary to feel guilty for not paying them back."

"You're funny."

Mimicking my mother by touching her hair, I ask, "Is there something you want to talk about?"

"When I was trying to sleep last night, I kept thinking about how you've never seemed so confident. I wanted you to know I noticed the change in you."

"Camden makes me feel okay being me."

Sally wants to tell me how I shouldn't need a man's approval to feel okay being me. She's dying to say it. I see her struggle with the words, and she finally wins.

"I'm glad you're happy together."

Now, I struggle with the words trying to escape my mouth. I desperately want to share with my family my marriage news. Like my mother, I triumph at keeping my mouth shut.

After Sally leaves, I feel alone in a quiet trailer park. Kids go to school. Parents head to their jobs. The elderly residents walk around at the nearby park. The stoners won't be up for hours. I'm alone with my cats and too much anxiety. I'm so tense I even consider exercising.

The sight of Camden sends me into tears. "I was stupid to want a night away from you."

"Not stupid," he says, wrapping me in his arms. "Simply foolish to think you could go a night without all this hot stuff at your fingertips."

Smiling, I know Camden is the one for me. Even if we crash and burn one day, all of the pain will be worth the happiness I feel now.

"Let's get married," he says after kissing away my fears.

We drive to Nashville to pick up our marriage license. I'm a ball of nerves again by the time we pull into the parking lot of the small church willing to marry us on short notice.

"My parents got married in this church," Camden says while we remain in the SUV. "Dad doesn't believe in weddings. I'm not his fanboy like Dayton, but Dad has a

190

point about the pomp and circumstance of an expensive wedding."

"I don't want a bunch of people staring at me."

"I don't want a bunch of people staring at you, either. I might need to poke out some guys' eyeballs. Wouldn't be romantic."

Grinning, I reach for the door handle, but Camden stops me.

"I got us wedding getup," he says, reaching into the back seat.

"I thought you said we weren't dressing up."

"I lied," he says, handing me a black T-shirt.

I unfold it to find printed in pink, "I love Camden and 1980s music."

Camden shows me his T-shirt with the words, "I love Daisy and 1970s music," printed in red.

"I thought to mention how my music taste was superior, but I figured today wasn't the day to rub that in your face."

"You just did."

"Only to show you how nice I am. I should still get credit."

Rolling my eyes, I can't stop smiling. "We're getting married."

"That we are."

"Do you think…?"

"I don't think, Daisy. I just do," he says, opening the door. "Don't make me steal your brain key."

Once inside, I retreat to a back room, where I change into the T-shirt. When I return, Camden is wearing his while standing next to the pastor.

Everything is kept short and straightforward. *I love him. He loves me. I want to marry him. He wants to marry me. Bam! We're husband and wife.*

"Missus Daisy Bourbon Rutgers sounds fucking perfect," Camden says back in the SUV. "I reserved us a room in a nice hotel."

Fanning my flushed cheeks, I mumble, "I thought we were going lowkey."

"I changed my mind."

"Is this how it'll be now, Mr. Bourbon Babe? You'll say one thing and then change your mind without telling me ahead of time."

"Yes. I'm a pain in the ass."

Smiling, I whisper, "You're my pain in the ass, though."

Camden cups my cheek and plants a kiss on my lips. I lean into him, sucking at his tongue.

"I want to fuck you right here," he growls when our lips part.

"Don't you mean you want our souls to touch through our crotches?"

"Yeah, that," he says, adjusting his jeans. "Don't say or do anything sexy until we're alone, or I can't promise my dick won't tear free and zero in on your tender spot."

I stare at him, saying nothing. My expression is blank. I try not to be sexy in any way, but I must sexily blink or breathe after we pull up to the hotel. Camden's gaze finds mine, and I think he'll pop free at any moment.

"We check in, go upstairs, and get you undressed."

"I'm not really in the mood," I tease before hurrying out of the car.

The valet takes Camden's keys. I see them exchange quick words, but my man's gaze is locked on me as I head inside. I walk to the front counter and try to hurry along the check-in process. The woman is friendly and wants to tell me every damn nearby place I could go for dinner.

"You have room service, right?" I ask her as Camden walks up behind me. When she nods, I tap the counter. "Check us in, please."

"Please," Camden whispers into my ear. "Your manners make me hard."

"I'll need to see Mister Rutgers's ID," she says, still taking her sweet time.

I turn to Camden and place my hands on his face. "I forgot to wear panties this morning. Will you please speed this thing the heck up?"

Camden steps around me, plops down his ID, and leans forward to whisper something. I don't know what he says, but her fingers type faster. A minute later, we have our keycards.

"Fancy," I say when he needs to use the keycard to access our floor. "You rich kids sure do live it up."

Once the doors shut and we're alone, Camden scoops me up and pins me to the wall.

"Tell me your pussy is already wet and willing," he whispers against my lips. "Tell me you're ready to be fucked because my dick is painfully hard."

"Will you cry if I make you wait?" I tease, wiggling my hips against his.

"No, but I might have to jack off waiting for you."

"No, no. I can't have you wasting a perfectly good erection."

Camden opens his mouth to speak, but the dinging elevator distracts him. As soon as the door opens, he effortlessly carries me down the hallway to our room. He unlocks the door and enters the air-conditioned room, where he lowers me on the bed.

"Naked, now."

"That's my line," I tease, kicking off my sandals. "Strip for me, Camden. Make me want you inside me."

Camden reveals an arrogant look as if he shouldn't need to do anything to make me want him. *Shouldn't his mere existence make me squirm?*

I pull off my T-shirt and cup my breasts still hidden under the pink bra.

"Show me," I murmur, and he removes his shirt. "I crave how your chest feels against mine. I love how hard my nipples get when they rub against your chest hairs."

"Fuck," he says, yanking open his jeans so his hard cock springs free. "Naked, now."

193

The sight of his dick in such a raging state brings out my merciful side. I strip down quickly and rest on my knees and elbows.

"Am I wet enough?" I ask.

"Not even close."

I open my mouth to tell him to try anyway, but the words turn into startled moans when his tongue licks me from clit to asshole. Camden is a starving man, devouring my tender pink flesh. The suddenness of such hot stimuli takes me over the edge quickly. Tearing at the blanket, I laugh at the guttural noises erupting from me as waves of pleasure ravage my body.

"I can't wait," he says as the head of his cock nudges open my wet folds.

"I'm not asking you to."

Camden sinks deep inside me and shudders with relief. "I love you," he says, and I look back so our lips can meet. "No one else will ever make me feel this way. Only you."

"Camden, I love you," I murmur. "You're my dream come true."

His hands grip my tits while his hips thrust harder into mine. Knowing his body now, I'm certain he won't last long.

I also know he'll want me again within minutes. The first time is only Camden warming up. The real show begins soon. I adore how well I've gotten accustomed to his body and needs. Even if I haven't learned everything yet, we have a lifetime to figure out the rest.

THIRTY FOUR - CAMDEN

Daisy is my wife. The words feel right in the same way saying I'm a member of the Serrated Brotherhood does. Some things fit perfectly in my life, and Daisy is the newest and best addition.

"Haven't you been to a hotel before?" I ask while she jumps on the bed nearby.

"No. Have you?"

Grinning, I wonder how many bare asses before mine sat in this chair. I might care more if a naked Daisy wasn't still bouncing on the king-sized bed. Her tits call to me, asking to be sucked.

My gaze lowers to her bruised inner thighs. I hate knowing I've caused her pain. But Daisy swears she bruises easily, and the fucking was worth it. I can smell her pussy on my fingertips, and my dick hardens from the scent.

Daisy turns away from me while bouncing, and I enjoy a nice view of her round ass.

"Fuck," I mutter, stroking my cock. "Are you doing that to get me hard?"

Daisy turns around and focuses on my dick. Carefully climbing off the bed, she walks to where I work at my erection.

"Is that all for me?" she whispers.

"I want to feel your pussy," I grunt.

Daisy turns around and bends over to give me easy access to her still damp flesh.

"This is *my* pussy," I say, sliding my finger inside her.

Daisy pushes back against my hand, taking more of me. "Yes."

Covering my cock with the juices from her warm pussy, I stroke faster.

Daisy reaches down to caress her clit, and I can't control myself any longer. I wrap my hands around her elbows and pull her back so her pussy lines up with my cock.

"Sit," I demand, desperate for relief.

Unsure how to obey, Daisy hesitates. I press the head of my cock at her entrance and tug her back against me. My dick fills her in a hard thrust.

"Oh," she groans, resting her back against me. "How does this work?"

I don't answer with words. My hands grab her tits and squeeze the nipples as my hips thrust upward. My touch makes Daisy whimper. She's still so new to pleasure. All her years masturbating didn't prepare her for what I need. When I take her, she can only hold on and enjoy what I give.

"Camden," she whimpers, realizing our position allows her to play with her clit.

I hear her laugh as the orgasm hits her hard and fast. My dick loves the way her pussy clenches and how hot her juices feel rushing down our thighs. Daisy's on fire, having found the perfect position for her need to stimulate her nipples and clit.

Refusing to let up, I fuck her hard through her orgasms. I pinch her nipples when she's close, and I don't stop twisting them until she's limp against me.

"Oh, Camden," is all she can say after another orgasm.

"You love me."

Twisting around so our lips can meet, Daisy answers me with a delicate kiss. I share her tenderness, even while my hips work frantically to find relief.

"I love you forever," she whispers.

With those four words, Daisy shoves me over the edge, and I come so hard inside her that I see fucking stars. I catch her smiling at my pained groans. She likes watching me break down in front of her. That's how fucking Daisy feels. As if I'm tearing down every wall I've ever built and showing her everything I am.

THIRTY FIVE - DAISY

Once Clara Hallstead hears of her son's marriage, she organizes a celebration. I wish I could skip the event and hide away with Camden. However, I know both of our families want to make a big deal out of what we'd like to keep lowkey. We got our choice of wedding. The least we can give them is one night to celebrate.

Preparing for the party, I yank free my ridiculous ponytail. I can't seem to get my hair to look decent, and I'm frightfully close to shaving my head to end the struggle. My sisters wait for me in the living room with their kids. Sally sits outside with Betty and Charlie. Everyone is ready to go, but my inability to beat my hair into submission is holding us up.

"I need a dang hat!"

Ruby grabs my wrist, startling me. "You need to simmer down your tantrum, young lady."

"Suck it, Mom."

"Listen to me," she demands, holding my face in her hands. "You need to chill. No one cares about your hair except you."

"You wouldn't say that if you were the one trying to make a good first impression."

"Camden is your husband. You've nailed that down, and your silly hair won't change things. Why pretend with his mom when she'll end up seeing the real you eventually?"

"How is calling my hair 'silly' helpful?"

"You're missing the point. Camden loves the real you. Stop acting like an insecure fool."

Smiling, I exhale my tension. "You're obnoxious when you're right."

"I know. Now brush your damn hair and get your ass dressed so we can go."

Once Ruby leaves me to do my final touches, I join Harmony in my bedroom. She encourages me to wear my favorite black-and-red tie-dye skirt, a black T-shirt, and polka-dotted socks.

"Feeling comfortable is a fundamental part of feeling confident," she says like a walking, talking bumper sticker.

"Will you be okay seeing Dayton?"

"Sure. I saw him the other day at the grocery store. I see him all the time. What's the problem?"

"Just asking."

"I'd have meaningless sex with him if I weren't certain he'd fall madly in love with me," she says, checking her hair in the mirror. "I just can't deal with the work involved in having a stalker."

"You're so rational."

"And you're so married."

Grabbing her hands, I jump up and down. "I'm married!"

Harmony laughs, but Ruby only pokes her head into the room and frowns. "Get moving, Bourbon."

"Leave me alone, Whiskey."

"Save the animosity for the in-laws," Harmony says, handing me the skirt. "Mom and the Hallstead family have a history."

"What?" I ask, startled to be hearing this now.

"They hung around in the same bars at around the same time. You know how catty women can be."

"Great," I mutter, pulling my shirt over my head. "What if they end up fighting?"

"My money is on Mom. Poor chicks hit harder."

Laughing, Ruby returns to the living room. She loves the idea of the Hallstead family getting smacked around. Even though she loathes Bonn now, she once loved him enough to hate his enemies. In her mind, his father's family are the bad guys.

Camden arrives a few minutes after I finish dressing as if sensing I'd run late. He smiles at my outfit before picking me up and sucking on my neck for everyone to see.

"Children are watching," Ruby grumbles.

"It's good for them to see a loving marriage," Camden grumbles back.

"What did he say?" Betty asks, and I sense an "us versus them" battle brewing.

"He said I'm awesome," I announce, climbing off my Viking. "Let's go before I have another hair meltdown."

Rather than holding the party at Clara Hallstead's house, we arrive at her older sister Alice's estate. The town sheriff lives the good life in a giant, purple Victorian. I've always hated the house, even though I love purple. I just don't get having a grape-colored home.

"I'm not sure how my uncle lives here without clawing out his eyes," Camden says, opening the car door for me. "It's purple inside, too."

"I'm sorry if I embarrass you tonight," I mumble, pulling him aside before we walk inside. "I'll try to keep my mouth in check. But I ramble when I'm nervous, which I'm sure you've noticed."

"Why be nervous? If Mom doesn't like you, what do I care? She isn't the one married to you. I am, and that makes me a happy fucking guy."

"You are happy, aren't you? So terribly happy and enslaved by me," I say, wrapping my arms around his hard body.

"I am enslaved. By the way, I might beat on Dayton tonight. He's jealous of what I have and insists on being an ass about it."

"Please don't fight with him at the party."

Camden glances around while trying to tamp down his temper. "He invited that twat JJ to our party. I'm ready to fucking kill Dayton right now."

"But you won't murder him, so let it go."

"I'll promise no fights if you promise no nerves."

"It's a deal. I'll pretend everyone I talk to is you."

"And I'll pretend Dayton isn't playing a game with me and the twat."

"Maybe he actually likes the twat."

199

Camden wears a horrified look. "That's so much fucking worse. I can't even imagine respecting him again if he finds anything even remotely likable about that fucking piece of shit."

Caressing his cheek, I softly suggest, "I know JJ's a thug, and you think he wants your club. Isn't it possible he wants to be close to his no-show dad? For him, being in Hickory Creek with Howler could be something he's wanted since he was a kid."

"He's a conman," Camden says, shooting down my attempt at humanizing his enemy.

"Okay."

"No, trust me, he is."

"Okay."

"I know what I'm talking about here. I'm a good judge of character."

"I agree."

Camden frowns at me, but I only smile and take his hand.

"If something pisses you off tonight, just take me aside and cop a feel. All of your problems will disappear once your hand is on my boob."

When I press his hand to my breast, he instantly squeezes.

"You can feel me up all you want too, babe," he says, lifting my chin so he can plant a kiss on my lips.

Ollie claimed he was too busy to attend the party, but I know he didn't want to see Sally or meet Camden. Though my dad bailed, I hear the rest of my family arrive.

"If my mom punches your mom, I'll make it up to you with a blowjob tonight."

"Same goes for if my mom nails your mom in the jaw. Oh, fuck it. I'll go down on you either way. I like the way you squirm when I lick your clit."

Balking at his dirty mouth when our mothers are close enough to hear, I wonder if tonight could go worse than I imagined.

200

Camden grins at my expression. "Anywhere we are, and no matter who we're with, I'm thinking about fucking you. If you get nervous, think of me wanting to stroke your pussy with my cock. That ought to distract you if copping a feel isn't an option."

"It's always an option," I whisper. "Even if I have to run across a room and tackle you."

Laughing, Camden takes my hand. His dick is likely rock hard, but he only has himself to blame.

Inside the house, I face a whole lot of people I don't know. Overhead, country music plays. The food looks and smells weird. *Yep, tonight is off to a rocky start.*

"Mom, you've met my wife, Daisy, before, haven't you?"

Clara is an effortlessly beautiful woman. She's also rather scary with her icy blue eyes.

"Welcome to the family," Clara says, hugging me tight enough to make my bladder whimper.

Camden narrows his eyes, but I'm unsure if he's giving me a weird look or his mom. His mom's long hug scares the shit out of me. Copping a feel from Camden has never been so appealing.

"Hello, Clara," Sally says, walking over to us. "Where's Alice?"

"Out back, showing off her lavender."

"How frigging fantastic," Sally says, shaking Clara's hand.

The two women keep shaking hands. They shake and shake and shake until I worry they're stuck. Camden's gaze is elsewhere, and I suspect the twat is already here. All I know is Sally and Clara have grossly overestimated the time necessary for a good handshake.

"We have a full bar for you to enjoy," Clara says, finally letting go of Sally's hand.

"You're too kind, but I only drink with friends."

Clara and Sally narrow their eyes at each other, and I wonder if they'll start shaking hands again. Before one of the moms throws a punch, Ruby pushes Chevelle in between the warring women. Nothing like a beautiful little girl decked out in a princess dress to cool tempers.

"Aren't you a doll?" Clara says, beaming at her great-niece, who bats her eyes.

Chevelle's shy with kids her age. But with adults, she knows how to work a crowd. Ruby smiles full of pride at how people coo over her baby. Bonn is nearby, also watching his daughter. I hope the two old lovers don't pay each other any mind tonight. The tension level is already too high.

"I want one," Camden whispers in my ear.

His arms wrap around me, and he pats my stomach. I think of a little person blessed with Camden's warm brown eyes and a half-smirk that'll turn any woman to mush. I'm in love with the idea of a boy or girl safe in their daddy's arms the way I am right now.

"I'll stop my birth control while you have a talk with your sperm."

"What would that talk sound like?"

"Everything before now was practice, boys. Now, you're in the show, so aim straight and steady."

Though Camden wears a smile, he's tense against me. I look back at Sally and Clara standing on each side of Chevelle. They're struggling to focus on my niece's cuteness rather than their mutual dislike. Before they can get into it again, Harmony appears with Keanu, who takes Chevelle's hand. I instantly feel ovaries quivering all around me from the cuteness overload.

"Bringing the kids was a smart idea," Camden says. "I'm still worried about them in the same place as my drunken family."

"No one's liquored up yet, and the kids have seen plenty of sloppy drunks before."

"Well, they do live in Lush Gardens," he teases.

"What's with the drama between you two?" Harmony asks Sally.

I glare at my sister and mentally will her to shut up, but she doesn't care. She's curious, and Harmony doesn't filter herself well.

"Back in the day," Clara says, full of indifference, "when I was dating Mojo at the beginning of our relationship, we saw other people. One of his hussies was Sally Slater."

"Eww!" I cry, staring horrified at Camden. "Your dad did my mom?"

"It's a small town," he says, shrugging. "Where's the self-respect in feuding over a man who hasn't nailed either of you in at least a decade?"

As I remain stuck on the eww factor from knowing Mojo sampled Sally's body, Camden's words affect the independent women. They study one another.

"Can't let a man stand in the way of enjoying my daughter getting married," Sally says, putting out her hand.

Nodding, Clara takes her hand. "I can't think of a finer woman for my boy than Daisy."

The women shake hands for the customary few seconds before letting go. I smile at their truce and then focus my beaming gaze on Camden.

"You're such a sweet talker."

"You sound surprised," he murmurs.

Leaning my head against his chest, I can't believe this remarkable man loves me. I don't know if I'll ever feel worthy, and maybe that's a healthy thing. I never want to take his love for granted. Camden's heart belongs to me, and I plan to keep it that way forever.

THIRTY SIX - CAMDEN

Daisy is a ball of nerves. Even after our mothers bury the hatchet and not in their backs like I initially assumed they would. I don't know why any woman discarded by my father would act like an idiot over his affections. Logically, I get how chicks find him attractive. Emotionally, I can't see how they'd put up with his shit for a hot minute. It's probably a good thing I'm not a woman with a thing for bad boy bikers.

Mojo arrives with several members of the club and their wives. I wonder why he thought to bring his enforcers to a wedding party. Mojo walks to me, shakes my hand, and says hello to Daisy.

"The food any good?" he asks as if we're at someone's barbecue.

"It's fine," I mutter. "What's with the muscle?"

"Ah, their wives wanted to feel included. You know how the old ball and chain can be."

Mojo says the last part while looking directly at Daisy. She doesn't shirk away from him as I expect.

"The food is stinking up the room," Daisy tells him. "And your muscles' shitty cologne ain't helping."

"You got a mouth on you."

"I'm married to your club's future president. Can't I complain about stink?"

When Mojo narrows his gaze, Daisy mimics him.

"The sad thing is if you win, you only beat a woman who can't fight," she says, still staring at him. "Not much of a victory for a man like you."

"I'll still take it," he says, adding real meanness into his glare.

"I bet that's the same look you have when you're working out a big dump."

Smiling at Daisy's cockiness, I don't know how she can be terrified of my mother yet ballsy with my terrifying father.

I suspect she grew up around too many strong women and not enough tough men.

"I'll let you have this," Mojo says, offering her a smile. "Consider it a wedding gift."

Daisy shrugs. "I'll let you pretend you weren't going to lose anyway."

"You're a funny chick," Mojo says, reaching out to tug at her hair.

My hand snaps out and grabs his wrist. "She's not yours to touch."

"You're too sensitive, son."

I refuse to release his wrist, even as he attempts to tug it away.

"Never touch her," I say, fighting my temper. "Save your flirting for bar whores. If I catch you giving her eyes, we'll have a problem."

"Will we now?"

Releasing his wrist, I shake out my shoulders. "I've hurt men for less."

"That you have."

Before I can feel too triumphant, Mojo glances around my shoulder. "Your brother and his new boyfriend are here."

"It's a scam," Daisy announces. "I bet Dayton is playing a long con with JJ, and you'll both be impressed by his ability to tolerate the twat. Never underestimate a man who looks like Camden."

Though Mojo laughs at her comment, I can barely keep from throwing her over my shoulder and finding an empty room in the purple house. My dick begs me to ditch the party. It doesn't care about keeping up appearances. The beast only wants to enjoy the smiling woman with the pretty pink pussy.

"You should be careful with Mojo," I whisper after my father wanders off to annoy Clara. "His view of women is old school."

"I'm more worried about him nailing my mom than anything he'll do to me. Eww," she says, shuddering. "Let's hope he washed up between our mothers."

Fighting laughter, I cup her face. "You're so fucking hot when you get grossed out."

"You're always hard," she says, casually patting my crotch. "I'll need to get better at blowjobs or quickies, so we can keep your dick under control."

"Yes, to everything you said. Let's sneak off."

"No," Daisy mutters, casually pushing me off.

"Why not?"

"Dayton and the twat showed up when you were intimidating your dad. You need to stick around to make sure they don't think they spooked you."

"I don't give a fuck what they think."

"Yes, you do."

I glance around until I spot Dayton and JJ chatting with Ruby and Chevelle. While the girl smiles at whatever they're saying, her mother only frowns at Dayton. I think she might punch him. He seems to notice her anger and puts up his hands defensively.

"Should I intervene?" I ask, suddenly unable to think for myself when Daisy is around.

"No. Let Bonn handle it," she says, pulling at my belt buckle. "He wants to. You can see him hanging around, watching what's happening. If you jump in, he won't. That guy really needs to grow a pair around the Hallstead family."

"You're a wealth of wisdom today."

Daisy gives me a bright smile. "I'm great at telling other people what to do. Running my life is the tough part."

"Good thing you married a controlling man."

"Oh, yeah," she teases and tugs at my shirt. "You can think for me. Tell me when to speak. And when to bend over and spread my legs for you."

"Bourbon Babe, if you keep teasing, I'm taking you somewhere private."

Daisy giggles as my wandering fingers slide under her shirt. One day, I'll learn to train my dick to behave. For now, I need to provide whatever it desires.

Sneaking into the house while everyone focuses on Bonn arguing with Dayton, I take Daisy into Aunt Alice's long-neglected workout room.

"I have an idea," I whisper against her lips while lifting her onto a little desk. "No time to get you good and ready."

"I can take a little pain if I get to watch you come undone."

Smiling, I unbuckle my jeans and shove them down. My dick is long past ready for relief, and I fist it roughly. Stroking my erection, I tug off Daisy's panties. Even in the dimly lit room, the curve of her pussy glistens. My finger slides between her flesh and finds her wet but not enough to welcome me comfortably.

Though I could take her hard like she offers, Daisy isn't ready for pain. She nearly cried yesterday when she tripped over the cat and fell hard on her tailbone. As desperate as I am, I won't make her shed a tear.

The head of my cock is slick with pre-cum. I slide my hard flesh against her soft opening, covering the folds with semen. Daisy closes her eyes, enjoying the rhythmic pressure against her clit.

I use my free hand to caress the hood of her clit and reveal her swollen pink nub.

"Camden," she whispers, squeezing her nipples through her shirt. "Fuck me."

I only smile at her begging. My cock wants to open her up. The head even dips inside her once, finding her hot and wet. Not enough for my size. Even weeks after our first night together, Daisy remains unbearably tight.

Thick pre-cum covers her flesh as I move faster. When I think of filling her with my cum and making a baby, my balls tighten. She's mine, and I know how to make her orgasm anywhere. Daisy doesn't even think of her family when I have her legs spread. Her knees tremble as I bring her closer to an orgasm. She'd come for me in front of an audience if I demanded it. In these moments, Daisy submits completely to me.

No one except me will see her so vulnerable. Only I'll ever open her up in this way. I'll be the man to coat her pussy in my seed.

Her body shudders from the orgasm my fingers elicit. I stare down at her and see a woman completely revealed. No one will ever know this Daisy. Or witness how she fearlessly meets my gaze even while her pussy remains on display for me to enjoy.

THIRTY SEVEN - DAISY

A married woman ought to live with her husband. Camden owns a charming condo with space for my various crap. I should pack up and move into his place, but I hesitate day after day. One packed box rests near the door. A second sits on the floor of my bedroom. Despite wanting to start my new life, I can't muster the interest to pack everything else.

A few nights a week, I spend at Camden's condo. Otherwise, he bunks at my place. We pretend this arrangement is reasonable. In reality, we know I'm afraid to let go of my home. My heart's always belonged in Lush Gardens.

"Don't cry," Ruby says, digging through my closet. "You'll be here every five minutes every day for the rest of your life. The only thing different is where you spend your nights with Camden."

I wipe my eyes and nod at her thoughtful words. Even if she wasn't right, I can't argue with a woman willing to give up her day off to help me pack. Harmony left for work hours ago while Sally went to bed after returning from the night shift. Once Ruby sees Chevelle onto the bus, she joins me to figure out what I should take and what needs to head to Goodwill. To make the tedious task more exciting, Ruby plays Madness singing "Our House."

"What happened between you and Dayton at the party?" I ask when we take a break after dumping half of my wardrobe.

"He was teasing me about not dating after Bonn. Basically, the ass was showing off for his ass friend."

"I heard Bonn and Dayton got into a shoving match."

"Yeah, it was kind of girly."

We share a smile. "Camden thinks JJ is a bad influence on Dayton. However, I believe Dayton's problems are separate from the new guy."

"I don't know any of them well enough to say. Hell, I don't even know Bonn. No way can I make observations on his cousins or half-brother."

"I should have stuck around and comforted you."

"Rather than having sex with your new husband?" Ruby asks, giving me a smile. "Yeah, I can see how you'd struggle with that decision."

For the next few silent minutes, Ruby and I drink juice at the kitchen table. I don't know what she's thinking, but I'm exhausted after seeing how many clothes I've held onto from high school.

"Do you think you'll ever get over Bonn?" I ask for maybe the millionth time since they broke up.

"If you lost Camden, would you get over him?"

"No."

"There you go. People always act like moving on is so great, but I'd rather be alone than be with anyone else. Guys like Dayton think I'm bitter toward men when I'm only accepting my options. I can settle for someone who will never measure up, or I can avoid romance. Dating is overrated, and I have a great life with my family."

"I know you miss being a bartender."

Ruby lost her old position when the Common Bend sheriff went rogue and decided to kill anyone who crossed him. She became one of the targets. Ever since, she's kept far away from Common Bend, even with a new sheriff around.

"Should I ask Camden for help finding you a new job?"

"Look, I like your loverboy, but I refuse to owe him anything. I'll find my own job. For now, waitressing pays the bills."

Her words make sense, but Camden's power infects me. He got me the job I wanted. Now, I see him fixing everyone's problems. This idea is ridiculous, but I've never known anyone with both power and a willingness to help.

"What did Ollie say about your marriage?"

"He wished me the best."

"Can't say much different, can he? He plays by the same rules as everyone else in Hickory Creek."

"Dad views himself as a 'law and order' man, but he's part of the same system as the rest of us. Some people always have power, and others never do. It's not necessarily fair, but it is what it is."

"Hey, now that you're living in the same building as Bonn, you can play chauffeur with Chevelle. That way, I won't have to see him even for a second."

I open my mouth to mention how facing Bonn more often rather than less might help her get over him. Before I can piss her off, our phones chime with a message from Missy Bumruck.

"RED ALERT! Man with bashed face headed to south end of park!!!!"

All her exclamation marks send me into a panic. Missy is Lush Gardens' self-designated guard dog. From her front trailer, she can see anyone entering from the main parking lot. If they so much as blink wrong, she warns everyone using a Facebook group. However, never before has she used so many exclamation marks.

Ruby rushes to the window and studies the quiet day. "I don't see anyone."

"Should I call Camden?"

"For what?"

"He bashed a guy's face in a while back."

Ruby only frowns at me. I don't know what to do. *Should I call Camden? Am I paranoid?*

"Send him a quick text just in case," she says, looking out the window again. "Maybe I should check on Keanu and Charlie."

"No, don't go out until we know what's happening."

I text Camden about Missy's message. He'll likely think I can't fart without informing him. He wouldn't be wrong, either. I tell him everything because nothing feels real unless he knows about it.

"Shit," Ruby mutters under her breath. "I think it might be your guy. He's heading this way."

"What do we do?"

"I don't know."

After texting Camden again, I run to where Ruby looks out the window. I recognize the man checking the addresses on each trailer.

"That's the one Camden beat up at the bar. I think his name is Lincoln."

"Then, we need to stay quiet and hope he goes away."

We peek through the curtains and watch him struggle to find a pattern to the addresses. Years ago, we moved several trailers around in the park. We weren't supposed to, but Sally wanted her girls to be closer to her. No one complained, so now the addresses don't line up.

I tiptoe to the kitchen and quietly dig through a drawer to find two knives. "Here," I whisper, handing her one. "We'll stab him to death and call it a day."

"Sounds easy enough."

"What if he has a gun?"

"Stab him faster."

Smiling despite my fear, I can totally picture myself kicking this guy's ass. We'll stab him dead, and Camden will clean up the body. *No muss, no fuss.*

As usual, reality proves more difficult than the fantasies in my head.

The next few minutes are painfully slow. Ruby and I watch him checking each trailer. He stops at hers for a long time since her number is similar to mine. After he peers through the windows, he gets frustrated and begins searching again.

Calling the cops never occurs to me. When trouble brews in the trailer parks and rundown apartment buildings, the local deputies tend to shoot first and clean up the innocent victims afterward. No doubt, they're less trigger happy when answering a call at a Hallstead home.

Though Camden is a Hallstead, the cops reporting to the park won't know or care about my husband's lineage. They'll assume everyone is a meth head with an illegal automatic weapon. The last time they came out to the park, they killed Gladys Markey's poodle when it bounced threateningly at them.

So calling the cops is out, and Camden hasn't answered my texts. I even wonder if he's okay. Did the butt nugget with the battered face hurt Camden before coming here? I have no time to send a third text before Lincoln stops at my trailer.

Ruby gestures for me to move back toward the second bedroom. She holds her knife at the ready. Mine trembles in my hand, but I have a good grip on it. If I need to, I can hurt someone.

I hear myself breathing. My beating heart is painfully loud. Every little noise feels like a scream meant to alert Lincoln to our presence.

His shadow lingers behind the curtained front door. He stands on my porch for what seems like forever. Just when I think he might turn and leave, the door flies open from a kick of his booted foot.

Running at him, I only want the jerk out of my trailer. Lincoln points his gun at me until realizing I'm an idiot with no plan. Before I can hack into his flesh, he grabs for the knife. On some level, I understand he doesn't want me dead yet. I don't care what he has planned. I'm all rabid dog reactions with no thinking involved.

Twisting my wrist, Lincoln forces me to release the knife. I break free of his grip and grab for his weapon with both hands. Struggling with him, I press his finger down on the gun's trigger. The first shot hits the ceiling. The next goes into the wall. By the time the gun clicks, we're firing into the ground.

"Bitch!" he yells, slapping me.

When Lincoln shoves me, my foot instinctually flies upward and nails him in the crotch. We both cry out. My tailbone slams into the hard floor while he cups his kicked balls. I assume the shot to the crotch will take him down, but Lincoln remains upright.

Ruby barrels into him like a pissed freight train. At five-seven, she's nearly as tall as Lincoln. They fall against the wall together, fighting over her knife.

I grab my weapon and crawl to where they struggle. Focusing on his leg, I imagine stabbing him. After a moment of hesitation, I plunge the knife into his thigh.

"Fuck!" he hollers, throwing Ruby off him and reaching for me.

I scramble back on the floor, leaving a trail of blood from the blade. He falls on top of me, pinning my body to the ground. I stab him once in the side before he knocks away the knife. His punch to my face shocks me. Why would anyone ever want to fight if this kind of pain is the result?

Ruby stabs Lincoln in the back twice before he grabs her and takes away the knife. He punches her next but can't get a second hit in before I dig my nails into his nipples. Even with his shirt to dull some of the pressure, he howls in agony. *Nipple pain apparently trumps a knife wound.*

Ruby slaps and punches him while he straddles me. I keep digging into his nipples. Whenever he lets go of her so he can hit me, she claws his eyes. When he lets go of me so he can stop her, I sink my teeth into his forearm.

"Bitches!"

Lincoln shoves Ruby away from him, and she tumbles onto the floor. He punches me but mostly hits his arm I'm gnawing on. Finally breaking free, he stands and moves to kick me. Ruby races at him, and they fall to the ground.

Crawling around again, I see the open door and wish we could run. Escaping alone isn't an option, so I scurry to my old TV. Picking it up, I toss the heavy relic at Lincoln as he stands after kicking Ruby off him.

"Fuck!" he yells as the TV crashes into his head and shoulder.

I run to Ruby and help her stand. She's bleeding, and I probably am, too. I only know we need to either kill him or run. So far, our fighting efforts haven't done much more than piss off the bastard.

Ruby grabs the kitchen chair and swings it at Lincoln. As he stumbles, I reach for my coffee table and throw it at him. Lincoln wipes blood from his forehead and glances between us. He likely realizes this battle is going nowhere fast because he reaches into his pocket to retrieve ammunition.

"Don't let him get the gun!" I yell.

The weapon ended up under the TV stand during the struggle. He runs for it, trips over one of my panicking cats, and goes headfirst into the wall.

I grab one of the knives on the ground and race to where he struggles to his feet. The blade gets him in the back of the neck. I imagine it plunging inside and killing him. Except the angle is awkward, and the knife leaves behind only a minor flesh wound. Lincoln turns to me, ready to swing a punch. I lower my aim and go for his crotch. His jeans blunt much of the strike, but he instinctually backs away to protect his balls.

Ruby appears next to me with a frying pan. "Fucker!" she yells, hitting him once and then again.

The pan meeting his head makes an awful thwacking sound, but he seems more bothered by my stabbing his crotch. I wish the knife were sharper, so I could do more damage.

We hit and stab him until his only move is to throw himself forward and knock us both down. I still have my knife and stab him in the face when he leans down to grab me. Ruby hits him in the knee with the frying pan. He lets out a yelp so earsplitting, the cats scramble from their hiding places and run to new ones.

Realizing my teeth did more damage than the knife seems capable of, I bite his arm. He growls something at me while knocking Ruby's pan out of her grip. He has us both by the hair and bangs our heads together. Even stunned, I manage to sink my teeth deeper into his arm.

"Motherfucker!" he hollers in pain, but I don't get the credit.

Still in his grip, Ruby manages to undo his pants, slide her hand inside, and find something worth squeezing. I've seen her destroy a lemon with her iron grip and don't envy his balls.

When Lincoln reaches for the knife, I imagine him plunging it into Ruby like I couldn't do with him. Letting go of his arm, I squirm free enough to kick him backward and away from the blade.

Ruby and I remain hunched on the ground while Lincoln struggles to regain his footing near the busted doorway. No one is ready to give up. I want Lincoln dead. I just don't know how to make it happen.

Standing, I pull Ruby to her feet, and we face our opponent. He readies for another round. I know he's thinking about the gun and whether he can grab it before we reach him. We never learn the answer.

A clunking sound startles me. Lincoln collapses on the ground. Behind him stands Betty holding a shovel. Sally appears next to her with an ax.

"We need better weapons," Ruby mumbles.

Lincoln surprises us all by going from limp to springing to his feet. Giving up on the fight, he barrels through Sally and Betty and disappears out the door.

"We can't let him get away. He could come back," I say, running after Lincoln like an idiot.

The four of us follow the wounded man's blood trail. Before we find him, I hear a gunshot ahead, and my courage disappears. *Did he kill someone because of me? Why couldn't I have stabbed him better? Why don't I have sharper knives? How come I never considered asking Camden to teach me to fight?*

When we catch up to Lincoln, he's kneeling in front of a sun-hat-wearing Charlie sporting a shotgun. Sally hurries over and pounds him with the flat side of the ax. He flops forward, and I suspect he might finally stay down.

"That's how we do it in Lush Gardens," Charlie says, still pointing her gun at the limp man.

Billy appears from the trailer with Keanu in his arms. He doesn't approach, knowing the women can handle the situation. Billy is an ace at fixing cars. He leaves fixing people to his wife.

"Who in the fuck is he?" Sally asks me.

I try to settle my raging heart. "One of JJ's friends."

"Who in the fuck is JJ?"

"One of Howler's kids."

"Brotherhood troubles in our park," Betty says, holding her shovel at the ready in case someone needs hitting. "Sounds about right."

Hugging Ruby, I ask if she's okay.

"You should see the other guy," she mumbles with a bloody mouth.

Inappropriate laughter bubbles up inside me. I'm not happy or amused. I'm mostly relieved and unable to process how I went from whining about moving to cannibalizing a stranger.

My mind is too numb to think of Camden. Or how much he might suffer once he learns a man he beat down came after me to get his revenge. When his heart is involved, Camden isn't rational. He can't think long-term. He lives in the present, and I suspect losing me would destroy him. So, I don't think about Camden or let myself text him, knowing I'll fall apart as soon as I hear his voice.

Until then, I laugh like a crazy person while figuring out what to do with the unconscious jerk in Lush Gardens.

THIRTY EIGHT - CAMDEN

Fucking traffic needs to fucking die! Old people, kids, cops, everyone in my way should fucking disappear so I can reach Lush Gardens faster. My mind shows me Daisy in various states of suffering. She needs me to protect her, but I'm not there. I'm speeding around slow-ass drivers with nowhere to go.

Daisy's texts paint enough of a picture to make me worry. When my response goes unanswered, I panic. Nothing matters except seeing her again. I'll kill anyone to save her. I'll give my life to let her live another day. I'm lost until I know she's safe.

Rather than stop when I reach the parking lot at Lush Gardens, I keep driving down the main pathway past one trailer after another. My mind is so set on Daisy's death that I nearly don't recognize her standing alive next to Ruby.

The Harley stops too suddenly, and I nearly take a header over the front. Recovering from my panicked stupidity, I climb off and run to Daisy. Even bruised and bloodied, she casually smiles at me. I sweep her into my arms and mutter something about killing whoever hurt her.

"Show me how to use a gun," she says when I let her go enough to examine her face. "Knowing that would have saved me a lot of trouble today."

Next to us, Ruby nurses a split lip. Nearby, Sally and Betty hold their makeshift weapons. Finally, I notice Charlie with her shotgun pointed at the unconscious guy on the ground.

Lincoln looks dead until I kneel enough to see the fucker's chest rise and fall. He's out cold, and even a finger shoved into his facial wound doesn't wake him.

"What in the hell happened?" I ask.

"He showed up and broke my door," Daisy says, sounding pissed about the damage to her place. She's clearly in shock. A woman who loses her shit over stubbing her toe should be wailing from the injuries to her face. "Ruby and I fought him. He wasn't expecting that, or else he would have shot us before we got the upper hand."

"How did he get out here?" I ask, wrapping his wrists behind his back and tying them with plastic restraints I carry around for situations like this one.

"Betty and Mom showed up, and he realized he was screwed. Ran out here where Charlie scared him. Not bad for a bunch of chicks, eh?"

Daisy's tone startles me. Her adrenaline is washing away, leaving her frightened. Ruby hugs her.

"What do we do with him?" Sally asks me.

"I'll call someone."

"You do that," she says, hugging her girls. Turning back to me, she sighs. "I was napping when the shit went down. I think I might just go back to that since you have things handled."

As Daisy and Ruby whisper to each other, I text Mojo to tell him to send enforcers to clean up what JJ brought to town. My new cousin might have no idea what Lincoln was capable of, and I'm the reason this fucker came looking for revenge. Nonetheless, I'm not beyond putting the blame on a guy I don't trust.

Daisy leaves her sister's arms and wraps herself against me.

"Once reinforcements show up, I'll take you and Ruby to the hospital and get you checked out."

"I'm all right."

"No, you're not," I growl.

Daisy isn't startled by my tone. She only looks up at me as if I'm behaving like a baby.

"I think I'm ready to move now."

Smiling at how she soothes me even in her terrified state, I know I've got the right woman at my side. Not that I ever had any doubt, but others did. After today, they'll back the fuck off about Daisy being too soft to handle my life.

THIRTY NINE - DAISY

Camden's condo doesn't feel like home even weeks after the move. My stuff easily fits in the master bedroom. The cats take over the spare room and hide under the guest bed for nearly a week. Even with all my belongings in the condo, I still view the place as Camden's bachelor pad invaded by furballs and their antsy owner.

Those days after the Lincoln attack, Camden treats me like a queen while I heal up from the bruises and a torn ligament in my left shoulder. I suspect this injury came from picking up my old TV.

"I need to learn how to fight," I tell him again one night as we rest in bed after sex.

Stretched out on his back, Camden glances at me and smiles.

"I'll make sure no one hurts you again."

"Do you plan to follow me around constantly?"

"I would if I could, but I have to leave you occasionally. I'll have someone act as your bodyguard."

"I don't like that."

"I know, but life is full of compromises."

Rolling on my side, I caress his sweaty arm. "I know you're the big man, and I'm your little wife, so what you say goes. Still, there's no way a butt nugget is following me around every day. You'll need to find a better plan."

Camden reaches around to pat my butt. "I can't be with you every moment."

"Teach me how to use a gun. If I shoot a few people, I'll get a reputation."

Camden laughs loudly, startling the cats from the room. My hubby loves the idea of me playing Dirty Harry in Hickory Creek.

"Man, would I get a load of whining from Mojo and Howler if my woman took shots at assholes."

I press the palm of his hand against my cheek. "I don't want to hide or have a sweaty man following me around. I know you're scared of me getting hurt, but I'm scared for you, too. Can I pay a douche to follow you around?"

"Why do you assume I'd get a sweaty douche to guard you? He might be a great guy, and you'll enjoy his company."

"What if I fall in love with him and leave you?" I ask, knowing I won't have to flash a boob to win this argument.

Camden narrows his eyes, and I feel his temper boiling. I struggle not to laugh at his angry reaction to my ridiculous scenario.

"No go. I'll hire a woman."

"What if I fall in love with her?" I ask, finally laughing. "I'm a very passionate woman."

Camden rolls over and wraps me against him. "Stop pushing my buttons."

"If I lost you for whatever reason, I'd return to Lush Gardens and live with my family there forever. No men, no dating, minimal masturbation. I'd never want to settle when I'd already enjoyed the best."

"I like that," he says, nuzzling my forehead.

"Would you replace me?"

"There's no replacing Bourbon Babe."

"Why?"

"You're you. When you smile, my life is good. When you frown, nothing matters more than making you happy again. I can't explain it any better than to say you own me. Nothing more complicated than that."

Camden covers my mouth with his and insists on more sex since I dared to mention loving imaginary people.

The nights are the easiest times for me. Whether we're at home or if we go out, Camden is always at my side. I don't miss my sisters, Sally, or Lush Gardens. I laugh easier. I don't worry so much about my new job. I'm comfortable in a way I'm not when Camden isn't nearby.

My mind often returns to the fight in my trailer. I imagine different scenarios where Ruby and I escape, or we kill Lincoln quickly. When my nerves get the better of me, I even think about Ruby dying.

Camden and I never talk about what happened to the loser. I didn't want to know. I was banged up and scared but also invigorated from surviving my first fight. As time passes and the bruises fade, I get curious about Lincoln's fate.

I fear to ask Camden about the asshole. When we're together, he's relaxed. When he's dealing with his club lately, he gets pissed. Mentioning Lincoln can't help, but the need to know nags at me.

"Where is Lincoln now?" I finally ask one night after crawling into his lap on the couch.

"Where he can't hurt anyone again."

"The entire town knows he attacked me."

"Fuck the town."

"You know what would be hardcore?" I whisper, kissing his jaw. "If we named our first son after him."

Camden looks at me as if I'm nuts. "How do you figure?"

"Rather than us being upset over what happened, we see it as a badge of honor."

"You have a strange view of the world."

"No, not really. Think about how everyone would know we gave our son the same name as the guy I survived and the one you handled. We didn't flinch. We won. He lost."

Camden studies me and then rolls his eyes. "You just like the name Lincoln."

"Well, there's that, too."

"People would think I was a royal asshole for naming my kid after that guy. They'd also think I was a little crazy. Couldn't hurt long term to have that reputation."

"People fearing you will keep you safe, and I want you to be with me until we're gray and saggy."

Camden kisses my neck. "Man, you'll make a sexy old chick."

"We're going to break so many hips together," I say, straddling him.

Camden kisses me for a long time before suddenly stopping. I worry my rolling hips injured something vital to making Baby Lincoln.

"I'll teach you to shoot a gun. Show you a few fight moves, but we're not pretending you're a badass. Believing a lie will get you hurt."

Smiling at how he's bowed to my will, I cup his face. "You're the badass in the family. I'm the voice of reason. I'm also the whiny one."

"I'm the nag."

"Oh, hell, yes, you are!" I cry, and Camden laughs. "If you weren't a boob man, I'd never win an argument ever."

Camden smiles at me, looking peaceful. Life outside our condo isn't simple. Here together with only the cats to break up our sexy times, Camden and I are the best we've ever been.

FORTY - CAMDEN

Lincoln swears he never told JJ about his plan to attack my woman. As much as I want revenge for what he did to Daisy and Ruby, there's only so much beating on a man I can do before I end up pitying him. Lincoln eventually begs me to put him out of his misery, and I do him the favor.

Dayton says nothing the entire time we dig Lincoln's grave. My brother and I have become strangers. I don't know how we reached this point in our twenty-nine years together.

"JJ told his guys to head back to Birmingham. He's staying here. They'll run their business without him."

"What exactly was that business?" I ask, standing over the now-covered grave.

"Nickel and dime shit. Don't worry about it."

Studying Dayton, I consider mentioning our current tension. We could talk out shit and hug and go back to how things were once.

Except we're different men now. I'm a husband. I have babies on the brain. I plan to take over the club, and no one will stand in my way.

Dayton is different too, but I don't know exactly how. He wants something out of reach. All his life, he's played the entertaining brother. Now, he isn't any fucking fun. He's someone else, and I don't like this guy. Not only because he's up JJ's ass. I just don't like how he looks at me as if I'm the interloper in his life.

"Thanks for the help," I tell Dayton.

He studies me like I did him. I wonder if we're thinking the same thing. We were once a lot alike. It's possible we still are.

Like me, Dayton chooses to let the topic die before uttering a word. We go our separate ways that day. I only see him in passing for weeks until De Campo's Pizza Shop burns down.

Standing across the street from the destroyed business, I assume the owner, Mickey, will likely take the insurance money and leave town. He isn't stupid and knows the club wants him out.

"Was this you?" I ask Dayton when he appears next to me.

"Mojo said to leave the business alone."

"What did Howler say?"

Dayton shrugs. "He talks a lot. Hard to keep it all straight."

"You know, one could view this fire as an attack on the club. We protected Mickey and his shop. Someone burned it down, anyway."

"I heard," Dayton says, scratching his new beard, "and this is just what I heard, but the fire was electrical."

"Oh, you heard that, did you? The place's still smoking, and you already got a cause. Someone is pretty fucking psychic."

"That's only what I heard," he says, smirking. "We'll see what the cops say."

Rolling my eyes, I walk away from Dayton. We both know how the local police work. If they think the club burned down the shop, the cops will protect us. If they believe our enemies burned down the shop, they'll look the other way so we can get payback.

Either way, the fire's cause will be ruled electrical. I don't care what the cops say. I know someone burned down the pizza shop. Only one person in town would have the balls to shit on Mojo's orders. Sooner or later, the same guy will end up in a grave near his buddy, Lincoln.

My father still runs the club. Until he hands over control, I can't do what needs to be done. So, I walk the line, follow orders, and watch my back.

Married life proves to be a welcome distraction from club drama. Daisy moves into my condo and starts her job at the White Horse school. We settle into our new life together, and everything happens easily. I never feel crowded by

225

having her in my place. Even her cats don't bother me, Yet, the condo does feel like my home rather than ours.

During the school's fall break, Daisy pukes up a hamburger. I instantly know she's pregnant. I think she knows too. However, we don't mention the obvious for nearly a month.

"Lincoln, if it's a boy," she announces. "Layla for a girl."

"I'm a man of potent sperm," I say, spinning her around.

"You'll make me puke."

"Wouldn't be the first time."

Daisy laughs even though I don't think she's kidding about her nausea.

"My Bourbon Babe is having my baby," I say, kneeling in front of her to kiss her tummy.

"Promise our baby can do whatever he wants for his future. You love the club, but promise you'll let our kids own their lives."

Looking up at her from my spot kissing her belly button, I smile. "My kids can do any fucking thing they want."

Daisy runs her fingers through my hair while I nuzzle her belly. Most evenings, I talk to the growing baby bump, and she plays with my hair. Every time I catch her gaze, I see the kind of love that strips me to my core.

EPILOGUE - DAISY

Working at the school, I finally have a career. I'm a professional woman with a skill set and respect from my colleagues. I love working with the kids, and the schedule allows me plenty of potty time when I'm pregnant with Lincoln. I thank Camden every day for getting me the job. *Well, until he asks me to stop because his ego is getting too big.*

Camden's confidence takes a big hit when the baby is born, and he realizes he's terrified of infants. Every time Lincoln cries, he gets pawned off on someone. Like with women's tears, Camden can't handle our child getting upset. He can change diapers and get up in the middle of the night for feedings. Crying, though, turns him into a panicked child himself.

By the time Lincoln is nearly a year, Camden is an ace father. He loves having a mobile kid rather than a living doll. Once our son can walk, Camden wants to teach him sports. I'm more interested in dressing up Lincoln.

My firstborn makes a fantastic impression of Billy Idol's snarl. Harmony notices this fact when Lincoln is six months, and I begin styling his hair into a faux-hawk. Camden thinks I'm weird, and he tries to sway our boy to the classics from the 1970s.

I hate leaving Lincoln to return to work. At first, I have a nanny in our place, but Camden doesn't like the woman and fires her on day one.

"She was casing the place," he claims.

We try having Charlie watch Lincoln, even though Camden swears our son comes home from Lush Gardens smelling like rednecks. I juggle the working mother routine for as long as I can. I love my job so much, but Camden wants me to stay home with Lincoln. He even promises I can teach Spanish to both him and our son, so my skills will stay sharp.

I give into his nagging once Lennox comes along. While our second boy lacks a Billy Idol snarl, he does scream in horror whenever The Rolling Stones come on. Camden only sighs and claims he'll teach them about good music once they're old enough to appreciate it.

The two boys keep us busy, but I get them on a solid schedule to allow plenty of alone time for Camden and me. My sisters and Sally babysit a lot. Clara also takes the boys every Friday, so I can enjoy karaoke while Camden trains with Erik and Hudson.

Somehow, our last baby comes along without throwing our routine into chaos. Layla fits comfortably into our family. She's so mellow that Mojo regularly claims she might not be "all there." Like any good mother, I sic my boys on their grandfather. Lincoln and Lennox think they're giving him love, but I know their little feet will always land in his crotch. Hell, Mojo even accuses me of training them to nail his balls.

"So, what are you going to do about it?" I ask, challenging him.

When Camden watches our bickering, I suspect his tongue will reward me later.

Layla isn't slow, but she is quiet. Her daddy says she takes after his brother, Hudson. Our little girl creeps around the house, scaring the shit out of people. Lincoln and Lennox learn early on to watch themselves around their sneaky sister. After all, her feet tend to nail them in the same spots as they nail their grandfather.

I often find myself amazed by how fast everything changed for me. One day, my car wouldn't start, and I ended up relenting to Camden's nagging for a ride. In a blink of an eye, I married the hottest, coolest man I've ever met. Suddenly, we were blessed with three kids who took after their daddy in the looks department and their mom when it came to musical taste.

I'm an indecisive woman, and I doubt I would have chosen this life. If left up to my wavering nature, I'd still live with my cats while pining over a man I nearly de-balled in a bathroom.

Fortunately, Camden takes what he wants in life and refused to take no for an answer.

EPILOGUE - CAMDEN

I'm not a patient man. As soon as Daisy heals up from Lincoln, I want another kid. Spreading the babies out never occurs to me. I always had Dayton at my side growing up, and I want my kids to experience the same closeness.

Lincoln does fine at the condo until he begins walking. Our balcony goes from a luxury to a hazard. The once spacious condo feels cramped with his toys and kid crap. With a second boy on the way, we need to find a house. I have a few in mind.

Except Daisy doesn't like the expansive ranch house. She isn't impressed by the split-level and a two-story with a big backyard. I don't know what Daisy wants until she stumbles upon it one day during a drive. That's when I'm forced to ask myself a very serious question. *How much do I love this woman?*

Daisy falls head over heels in love with the ugliest fucking house I've ever seen. Okay, maybe a few abandoned shacks in Hickory Creek look worse, but I've never seen a well-kept home as hideous as the one my woman creams her panties over.

"Why?" I ask in horror.

"It's very 1980s," she says of the blocky, brown contemporary eyesore.

"Exactly."

Her brokenhearted expression ends the discussion. *This monstrosity is our new home.*

Despite all the sharp edges outside and unsightly 1980s touches inside, the house weirdly fits us. The fenced yard also allows Lincoln to run himself into exhaustion.

Daisy agrees to change the wood siding from a shit-brown color to a dark blue. Otherwise, she insists on keeping the current character, especially the two-story stone fireplace atrocity.

Once we move in my furniture and her décor, the house makes sense. I don't even see the things I hate by the time Lennox is born. Soon, our life falls into a comfortably hectic routine with kids, cats, and even a dog.

Every morning, I run errands for the club. Daisy always sees me off while Lincoln rests on her hip, waving and giving me a snarl. The kid has a definite rocker vibe, even if his taste in music suffers from listening to Duran Duran for nine months in utero.

A year later, Lennox takes his brother's place as they see me off in the mornings. By the time Layla comes along to claim Daisy's hip, I contend with sons begging to ride with me. Plus, our new mutt barks wildly at the squealing boys.

Daisy wasn't what I expected. I fucked up the night of the party and nearly lost the woman who would change my life. I got my shit in order and won her heart. Now with Bourbon Babe at my side, nothing can stop me.

THE END

Printed in Dunstable, United Kingdom